"Merrie and I are getting married,"

Logan suddenly announced.

Without dropping a beat, he put his arm around Merrie's waist, pulled her close and kissed her astonished mouth.

A startled murmur rippled through the crowded yard—whispers of "Did you hear that?" and "How romantic."

Married?

Furious, Merrie pushed at Logan's chest without success. *The miserable rat*—he was just having fun at her expense. Still…she couldn't keep from moaning at the heat of his kiss.

It wasn't wise to get near him. She was too vulnerable…her body too responsive to his warmth and strength.

As soon as she was free, she'd throw Logan to the wolves.

Yet when his grip loosened, Merrie couldn't help clinging to his shirt. Her knees felt funny—sort of as if they belonged to a newborn calf.

"I'll get you for this," she whispered.

Dear Reader,

In May 2000 Silhouette Romance will commemorate its twentieth anniversary! This line has always celebrated the essence of true love in a manner that blends classic themes and the challenges of romance in today's world into a reassuring, fulfilling novel. From the enchantment of first love to the wonder of second chance, a Silhouette Romance novel demonstrates the power of genuine emotion and the breathless connection that develops between a man and a woman as they discover each other. And this month's stellar selections are quintessential Silhouette Romance stories!

If you've been following LOVING THE BOSS, you'll be amazed when mysterious Rex Barrington III is unmasked in *I Married the Boss!* by Laura Anthony. In this month's FABULOUS FATHERS offering by Donna Clayton, a woman discovers *His Ten-Year-Old Secret.* And opposites attract in *The Rancher and the Heiress,* the third of Susan Meier's TEXAS FAMILY TIES miniseries.

WRANGLERS & LACE returns with Julianna Morris's *The Marriage Stampede.* In this appealing story, a cowgirl butts heads—and hearts—with a bachelor bent on staying that way. Sally Carleen unveils the first book in her exciting duo ON THE WAY TO A WEDDING... with the tale of a twin mistaken for an M.D.'s *Bride in Waiting!* It's both a blessing and a dilemma for a single mother when she's confronted with an amnesiac *Husband Found,* this month's FAMILY MATTERS title by Martha Shields.

Enjoy the timeless power of Romance this month, and every month—you won't be disappointed!

Mary-Theresa Hussey

Mary-Theresa Hussey
Senior Editor, Silhouette Romance

Please address questions and book requests to:
Silhouette Reader Service
U.S.: 3010 Walden Ave., P.O. Box 1325, Buffalo, NY 14269
Canadian: P.O. Box 609, Fort Erie, Ont. L2A 5X3

THE MARRIAGE STAMPEDE

Julianna Morris

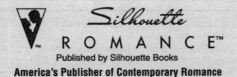

Silhouette

R O M A N C E™

Published by Silhouette Books

America's Publisher of Contemporary Romance

To my friends, Vicki and Carol,
who listened and believed.

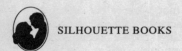

SILHOUETTE BOOKS

ISBN 0-373-19375-0

THE MARRIAGE STAMPEDE

Copyright © 1999 by Martha Ann Ford

Printed in U.S.A.

Books by Julianna Morris

Silhouette Romance

Baby Talk #1097
Family of Three #1178
Daddy Woke Up Married #1252
Dr. Dad #1278
The Marriage Stampede #1375

JULIANNA MORRIS

has an offbeat sense of humor, which frequently gets her into trouble. She is often accused of being curious about everything…her interests ranging from oceanography and photography to traveling, antiquing, walking on the beach and reading science fiction. Choosing a college major was extremely difficult, but after many changes she earned a bachelor's degree in environmental science.

Julianna's writing is supervised by a cat named Gandalf, who sits on the computer monitor and criticizes each keystroke. Ultimately, she would like a home overlooking the ocean, where she can write to her heart's content—and Gandalf's malcontent. She'd like to share that home with her own romantic hero, someone with a warm, sexy smile, lots of patience and an offbeat sense of humor to match her own. Oh, yes…and he has to like cats.

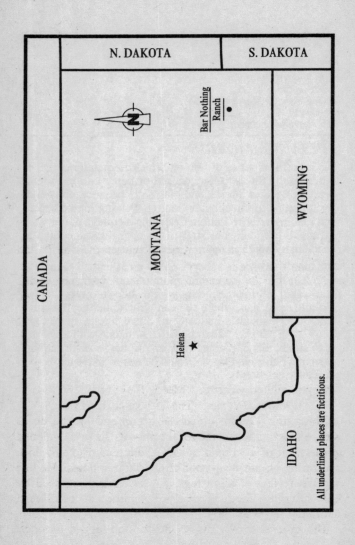

N. DAKOTA

S. DAKOTA

WYOMING

MONTANA

CANADA

Bar Nothing Ranch

Helena ★

IDAHO

All underlined places are fictitious.

Chapter One

"What now?" Logan Kincaid muttered as he pulled into his driveway.

A group of children were gathered beneath one of the big-leaf maple trees that shaded his property. They stared into the branches with rapt attention.

"Is something wrong?" he called and they jumped.

One of the boys faced him with a wary expression. "Our kite got stuck, sir. Merrie got it for us, but now she can't get down."

Logan sighed wearily. "Merrie?"

"You know, *Merrie.*" The kid rolled his eyes.

Shrugging, Logan joined the group and looked up as well, expecting to see the local tomboy. His eyes widened at the sight of a woman in shorts and a camisole T-shirt, squirming on the steep roof of the old tree house. He had a perfect view of silky legs, a bare midriff exposed by her struggles, and a nicely proportioned bustline... definitely *not* a tomboy.

His taste normally ran to sleek, long-legged blondes,

but "Merrie" was rather attractive. Actually *very* attractive. She radiated a healthy sexuality that made him think of a hot fire and mulled wine.

Stop that.

Logan stomped on his baser male instincts. This wasn't the time nor the place to admire a woman's innate appeal. And it wasn't as if he didn't already have enough female trouble—his boss's daughter had decided it was time he got married...*to her.* The thought sent a cold shudder down his spine.

"Er, I'll take care of this," he told the children. "You go on home."

They looked at him doubtfully and Logan winced. He had a reputation as the Ogre of Nisqually Drive. It was his own fault; he wasn't good with kids. He should never have bought a house in such a family oriented neighborhood, but it represented everything he'd never had. There weren't too many dirt poor kids who could grow up and buy million-dollar acreage overlooking the Puget Sound.

With great reluctance they trudged away, leaving only a sandy-haired boy. The lad had a mutinous look on his face, a wordless determination to face the ogre.

"Hey, Merrie," the boy called. "Thanks for getting our kite. Are you sure you don't want us to call 911? It's great when the fire truck comes. They turn on the lights and everything."

"No, I'm fine. Go have fun." She waved her hand.

The child cast another dubious glance at Logan. "I'll come back later and see if you're okay," he assured before following his friends. He obviously didn't trust an adult's ability to handle the situation. At least not *this* adult.

"What's wrong?" Logan asked the woman. "Why can't you get down?"

"Uh..." She looked down and he got an impression of jade-green eyes between strands of cinnamon hair. "You must be Mr. Kincaid."

He nodded.

"Hi. I'm Merrie Foster, Lianne's sister."

Another smile twitched the corner of his mouth. Lianne Foster was a quiet young woman who catered his dinner parties and cleaned his house three times a week. She seemed completely opposite to the disheveled firebrand fifteen feet above him. "Pleased to meet you. Why are you here, instead of Lianne?"

Merrie shifted, using her feet to shimmy upward a few inches. The rickety roof of the tree house creaked ominously. "Well...Lianne was supposed to get married next month, then she discovered her slimeball fiancé was sleeping with someone else. He's a real scuzz. Of course, the whole family knew what he was like except Lianne— she's a little naive when it comes to things like that. She always believes the best in people."

Logan blinked, fascinated by the roundabout explanation. "I see."

"I had him pegged immediately," she said confidentially. "They weren't engaged yet, but a decent man doesn't try to grope another woman when his girlfriend isn't looking."

"The scuzz groped you?"

"He tried, but I stabbed his hand with a fork." Merrie appeared quite pleased with the memory. "I think I hit a vein."

"Oh." Logan didn't know whether he should offer his congratulations or review the coverage on his health insurance. "How did Lianne take the news?"

Merrie pushed her hair away from her face and wrinkled her nose. "He told her it was all a misunderstanding and how *terribly* sorry he felt about everything and that it was all his fault—which of course it was, but he sounded *so* sincere and innocent. It was disgusting.''

Logan shook his head. "She believed him?''

"Yeah,'' Merrie said, annoyed. "Then she took him to get a tetanus shot.''

"Uh, a wise precaution.''

"It was a clean fork,'' Merrie protested. "Right out of the dishwasher. We hadn't started to eat yet.''

Pain twinged in his temples and Logan rubbed his forehead. It had been a frustrating week and all he wanted was some peace and quiet. But peace seemed out of the question under the circumstances. "Do you always tell total strangers about your personal business?''

"We're not total strangers. Or least we wouldn't be if you weren't so stuck up.''

He glared. "I'm not stuck up.''

"Huh.'' Her eyes narrowed. "I know all about it. Lianne invited you to Christmas dinner last year, but you refused even though you didn't have any plans with your family. Then she kept worrying about you sitting alone in that great big house for the holiday. Jeez, it's not like she was trying to seduce you or anything. She was just being friendly.''

"I never…that's absurd,'' Logan growled. "I didn't think any such thing.''

"Better not,'' Merrie warned. "Lianne isn't your type. She wants a lot of kids and a husband who'll spend time with her instead of trying to become the highest paid investment guru in the state of Washington. You wouldn't do at all.''

Logan ground his teeth. This was a ridiculous conversation, and it was getting more ridiculous by the minute. "Lots of people don't want kids. That doesn't make me the scum of the earth, just honest. How about you? Do you *really* want a bunch of rug-rats interrupting you every five seconds?''

"I love kids,'' Merrie said, then wrinkled her nose again. "Well...except at the end of the school year. You see, I teach *junior high school.*'' She uttered the last part in a dire tone of voice that suggested contact with adolescents was an extremely effective form of birth control.

"Oh.''

Merrie absently combed her hair with her fingers and braided the heavy length. "I have the sixth-grade class. They're still a little innocent at that age, but seventh and eighth are the worst. You know, I think teenagers are a different species entirely.'' She looked at the end of her braid and released the unbound plait. "What do you think?''

"I think you should get down from that tree.''

"I've been trying to...what do you think I've been doing all this time?''

"I wouldn't know.'' Logan rubbed the back of his neck. "If you had any sense you would have given those kids ten bucks for a new kite, or just told them to forget it. The children in this neighborhood aren't exactly deprived.''

If possible, her expression turned frostier. "Money isn't everything—they made that kite themselves. They're terribly proud of it.''

"Whatever. But what's wrong now?''

She shimmied upward again, wedging her bare foot on a tree branch extending over the roof. "I'm stuck.''

"Stuck?''

"Stuck. As in pinned. Caught. Unable to get loose.''

He waited—one eyebrow raised—until she sighed.

"I slipped and the back of my shirt got caught between

some rotten boards. But it isn't all bad, it kept me from falling off.''

"Tear it. I'll buy you a new one.''

She gave him an are-you-kidding-or-just-stupid? look. "I tried, but this knit stuff just stretches.''

"Then take it off.''

"No.''

With a stubborn expression on her face, Merrie wiggled again, reaching both hands around her back and tugging with all her might. The ancient tree house shuddered as she squirmed and Logan hovered between alarm and appreciation. The shirt kept edging up her stomach, exposing more and more skin—no wonder she didn't want to take it off...she wasn't wearing a bra.

"You'd better stop,'' he said. "This is supposed to be a family neighborhood.''

Merrie paused, composing a withering remark in her head. "Family? Huh. As if you cared. I don't—'' The words strangled in her throat as she realized what Logan Kincaid meant...her top had remained stationary, but her body hadn't. With a gasp she wiggled upward again and yanked the hem over her stomach.

This was awful. She couldn't remember the last time she'd been so embarrassed. Modern, intrepid women did not get into silly predicaments. And they didn't blush, especially in front of stodgy businessmen who saw everything in terms of profit and loss. Just the same, the unmistakable heat of a blush was crawling across her face.

"You were saying?'' he asked smoothly.

"Go away.''

"Easier said than done. You're stuck in my tree. Need any help?''

Merrie lifted her chin. She'd do what every independent woman should do in a similar situation—bluff. "I'm just fine. I'll manage."

"What are you going to do? Wait until dark and hope the neighborhood boys don't have flashlights? I'm sure they'd enjoy the lesson in human anatomy."

Her toes curled. At the moment, she *truly* disliked Logan Kincaid. She hated cleaning his already immaculate house, trying to substitute for her heartbroken sister. She disliked the way he'd turned a lovely home into a sterile status symbol. And she especially disliked *him*.

Oh, yeah?

Merrie cringed at the clamor of her feminine instincts.

Okay. So Lianne hadn't mentioned that her stuffy, uptight client had broad shoulders and a gorgeous voice. Imagine, failing to mention he looked better than Clark Gable and Cary Grant rolled up together.

Big deal. Lots of men had sexy bodies and great voices. *Nice* men. Different men from Logan Kincaid, whose idea of a good time was poring over a stock portfolio. Still, Merrie had envisioned him as a boring overachiever with a perpetually annoyed expression on his face. Not...*this*.

Not pure heartthrob.

Not a guy driving a flashy little Mercedes convertible. It was still a prestige car, but a lot more fun than a sedan. The men she knew didn't drive prestige cars—fun or not. They drove foreign economy models or old pickup trucks, being mostly teachers and cowboys. Lianne kept saying she should get out more, but Merrie had a schedule that didn't include a lot of time for socializing.

"That's a very strange expression," Logan called up to her. "Are you all right?"

No. I'm having an attack of lust, she thought, totally disgusted with herself. Brother, she had to get a grip. This wasn't only embarrassing, it was silly. Lianne's house-cleaning client might have the body of a matinee screen idol, but he was pure poison for someone like her. She wanted someone who enjoyed the country and animals and kids, and didn't care if he made a billion dollars by age forty.

Besides, he couldn't *actually* look that good. It had to be an illusion.

"I'm coming up."

"Don't bother…" Merrie's protest petered out because she didn't have a lot of options. She'd climbed up, confident of her ability to rescue the kite and get down. She hadn't contemplated getting caught like a treed cat. "Well…be careful," she said lamely.

Wood scraped against bark as the ladder was adjusted against the trunk. A few seconds later Kincaid swung onto the top of the tree house with surprising ease and he inched across the neglected structure. When she didn't move he lifted an eyebrow at her.

"Something wrong?"

Yeah. Everything.

The breath had whooshed out of Merrie's throat as though she'd been hit with a sledgehammer. *Blast.* Not only did Logan Kincaid look fabulous face-to-face, but he also looked…likable. Kind of tired and bored with life, but also endearing with a slightly crooked line to his teeth and little crinkles at the corners of his eyes. Her sister was right, she *should* get out more.

"I'm…I'm fine," she stuttered.

"Okay. Lift up a little so I can get you loose."

With bemused obedience, Merrie turned so he could put his hand beneath her back. The contact of warm, hard fingers against her skin created another shock and she closed her eyes. It was better that way. Safer, because she couldn't see him. Of course, she could still smell him.

God, he smelled great.

Merrie shook her head. This was crazy. Lianne had encountered a couple of his girlfriends over the years; she'd described each one as sophisticated, elegant, and possessing the personality of a dead mackerel. He even had a list of the characteristics he wanted in a woman, taped to his bathroom mirror. Merrie Foster—small town junior high-school teacher—*definitely* wasn't his type.

"You're sure stuck," Logan muttered as he tugged at the T-shirt. To get a better grip he bunched it in his fist, dragging the hem up her stomach again.

Merrie tried to pretend it didn't matter. Her breasts were cupped by the soft fabric. They were mostly covered except for the rounded underswell, and the tiny front buttons were too closely spaced to gape. Besides, Kincaid didn't seem to notice her impending exposure. Now *that* irritated her. She might not be his type, but she wasn't chopped liver, either.

"You're right, this stuff doesn't like to rip," he muttered. "And if I pull too hard we could both go flying."

She peeked beneath her lashes and saw a look of electric concentration in his brown eyes. He nudged her hip with his knee and she bit her lip. *Hard.*

"Uh, do you have a knife?" Merrie mumbled, feeling a little desperate. She'd never felt such heart-fluttering attraction in her life. It was embarrassing. Silly. Sophomoric. She was a twenty-nine-year-old woman, for heaven's sake! Almost thirty, though she didn't like thinking about that despised birthday.

"No knife," he said, frowning in concentration. "Maybe it will help if I pull up, instead of out."

He nudged her again and she almost screamed. She

should have let the kids call 911; a fireman in full gear would have been lots better than Logan Kincaid in jeans and a faded shirt that fit like a second skin. How could Lianne have spent four years doing his housekeeping and cooking for his dumb parties without experiencing meltdown?

"This isn't working," she said distinctly.

"I know. I'm going to give it a good yank, but I want you to hang onto that tree branch, just in case." He shifted position again, gathering the back of her shirt with both hands.

Merrie hooked her arm around the branch, telling her overheated mind to forget the show of concern for her safety. Kincaid was just worried about his homeowner's insurance. He didn't want a claim for injuries if she fell on his property; it wouldn't look good and would raise his premiums.

"Here goes," he murmured.

He yanked and the crack of splintering wood filled the air. The tree house roof disintegrated instantly and Merrie lost hold of the branch as they crashed down. With a powerful twist of his body, Kincaid rolled in the air to avoid landing on her. Instead she landed on *him* in an ignominious heap. Luckily the floor was a lot sturdier than the roof.

"*Umph*," she gasped, trying to get oxygen into her lungs. She wasn't sure if hitting the ground wouldn't have been softer. Logan Kincaid had a hard, fit body without an excess ounce.

"Are you all right?"

Putting her hands on his shoulders, Merrie pushed up to look at him. The rat didn't even look startled and he was breathing just fine. "I'm...*phhft*...dandy."

"Anything hurt?"

"L-like my pride?" she asked, still breathless.

The corner of his mouth twitched. "I was thinking more along the lines of cuts and bruises and broken bones."

"Oh..." Merrie shrugged. "Nothing to worry about. During the summer I normally work as a wrangler on my grandfather's dude ranch. I'm used to stuff like this."

His gaze drifted down. "That's interesting. *Exactly* like this?"

"You know...it happens. Falls and tumbles of various kinds. Even the best riders get thrown."

"I see."

Abruptly Merrie realized the intent of his question and she plastered herself to his chest again. Her pride wasn't the only thing she'd injured—her T-shirt had disappeared completely. But the worst part was the temptation to take advantage of the situation and discover if Logan Kincaid kissed as good as he looked. Men were fairly predictable, after all. He probably wouldn't mind a taste, even if she didn't meet his basic qualifications.

Ugh. Merrie gave her forehead a mental slap. If nothing else, that fall had done serious damage to her common sense.

"Where is it?" she asked, her voice muffled against his shoulder.

"Five feet up. It's stuck on what's left of the roof."

She cautiously turned her head and saw the ruined remnants of her shirt hanging above them. The buttons had apparently popped in lieu of ripping the back.

"Swell." Dust filtered down from the gaping hole and she sneezed. "Lianne owes me big time for this."

Logan's teeth gleamed whitely in the dim light. "Don't worry. You can wear mine."

His fingers slid between them, tickling her bare skin

as he unbuttoned the bottom of his shirt. He had two popped open before Merrie could think clearly and comprehend the direction he was taking—a little higher and he'd be tickling more than just her ribs.

"No, you don't, buster." In a single motion she rolled to the floor and turned her back. She crossed her arms over her breasts and scowled at the wall.

"That's gratitude for you."

"The longer I live, the more I realize that men are all alike," she announced.

"Ah, Methuselah talking. The wisdom of the ages."

"Very funny."

"Isn't ranch work a strange occupation for a teacher?" he asked. "You're a, um, you seem a little too small," he said, apparently qualifying his original thought, which undoubtedly included a reference to the fact she was a woman and shouldn't be doing a man's job.

Merrie scowled harder. "You sound like my grandfather. When I was a kid we spent every summer at the ranch. Then one day he realized I was growing up and decided I should be assigned to the cookhouse instead of riding fences. I had to burn four pots of chili and put salt in the coffee before he backed down."

The shirt, still warm from his body, settled over her shoulders and she stuffed her arms through the sleeves. It hung on her like a tent, but she tied it securely at the waist. She turned around and tried to ignore the sight of Logan's firm muscles and flat stomach. A wedge of brown hair on his chest tapered into a narrow line, disappearing into his jeans—which just made her wonder how he'd look without those jeans.

Lord…she was out of her mind.

He grinned and leaned back. "Do you hate all men?

Or just those of us who are old enough to notice women, and young enough to do something about it?''

Merrie blinked and took a calming breath. "I don't hate men. I've known a lot of louses, but I haven't given up on the sex completely."

"I haven't given up sex, either."

She gave him a repressive stare—the kind she usually reserved for unruly students. "That isn't what I meant."

"You mean you *have* given it up?" Logan shook his head, enjoying the furious flash of Merrie's green eyes. Damn, she was feisty. A lot of women would have been hysterical after nearly breaking their necks. "You might want to rethink that choice. As activities go, sex has a lot to offer. And it would be a shame to waste your equipment." He gave her a significant glance. "If you know what I mean."

"You...I...you're impossible." She kicked him with the heel of her foot and scrambled to the door of the tree house. "My 'equipment' is none of your business."

Additional light poured in through the open door and Logan frowned as he looked at Merrie. "Wait a minute, you're bleeding."

She hesitated, one foot on the ladder. "I'm fine."

"You need first aid."

"Huh...I know a line when I hear one. You should know that sexually harassing an employee is against the law."

"Lianne is my employee, not you," he pointed out helpfully.

"Excuses, excuses." She descended rapidly from view.

Logan sighed and followed, catching her halfway up the driveway. "It isn't a line. You're really bleeding."

He touched a spot on her lower back and she winced.
"See?"

Merrie shrugged when he lifted a red-stained finger.
"I must have scratched myself when I fell the first time."
A screeching noise sounded from the house and her eyes
widened. "But I don't have time for that."

"Make time."

"Not unless you want to call the fire department.
That's your smoke alarm. I'm sorry, I forgot. I...I left a
cake baking. It's probably charcoal by now."

"Damn!" Logan sprinted around the back of his
house. A thread of smoke rolled from the kitchen as he
ran inside. He grabbed a towel and kicked the oven door
open, then fished for the burning pan. "Get away," he
shouted to Merrie and flung the smoking mess as far into
the yard as possible.

They opened the windows to air the house, then rushed
outside again and collapsed on the grass. Merrie stared
at the charred remains of her culinary disaster, a funny
expression on her face. "It didn't rise."

"What?"

"Look—it's flat. Completely flat. Aren't cakes supposed to be high and fluffy?"

"Theoretically." Logan rubbed the back of his neck.
"What the hell difference does it make, anyway? It's
toast now."

"I just wondered." Merrie played with the tied ends
of her borrowed shirt. "Lianne said she always makes
you a cake on Wednesdays, so I tried to bake you a cake.
I hate cooking."

"You shouldn't have," he said with feeling. "I could
have survived without the cake."

Merrie gave him an irritated glance. "I promised
Lianne. She says it makes the house smell homey and

all. Honestly, she thinks you need mothering or something.''

Logan smiled. ''What do you think?''

Merrie wiggled her toes. She could get arrested for what she thought. ''I think you're a compulsive workaholic.'' *And sexy as hell.* If she hadn't been raised with old-fashioned values she probably would have attacked him by now.

''That isn't very nice for someone who tried to burn down my house. I take it you and Lianne aren't alike in the, uh, domestic arts department?''

''Hardly.'' She slumped backward and wrinkled her nose. ''During the year I teach science, and I spend the summers in Montana riding horses and tending cattle. I can cook the fluffiest biscuits and the best cowboy stew you've ever tasted...as long as it's over a campfire.''

''Well, you got the fire all right.''

Merrie hunched her shoulders. ''If you'd gone on vacation like you were supposed to, I wouldn't have been baking a stupid cake. I'd be in Montana right now, enjoying myself.''

''You're saying it's my fault?''

''Well...sort of. Lianne *really* needed to get away and do some thinking—you know, about her busted engagement and what she wants to do with herself. Of course, if it was me I would have been glad to have gotten rid of the louse. But then, I wouldn't have gotten engaged to such a creep in the first place.''

''Er, I don't suppose so.''

''Anyway, Lianne had everything worked out to cover for her clients. Except you, because she thought you were going out of town. Then you canceled and she couldn't get anyone else but me. I said she should just tell you to forget it, but she was so upset it didn't do any good. It's horrible. How could you cancel a vacation?''

''That's what I want to know,'' a chilly voice announced. ''I waited in Cancún for three days and you never arrived.''

Logan looked at the woman standing at the edge of his lawn and shuddered. Gloria Scott—the husband-hunting maven of the Pacific Northwest—had found him.

That's all he needed.

Chapter Two

Sophisticated and elegant.

Lianne was right about Logan Kincaid's taste in feminine company—the newcomer qualified in every aspect. Still...Merrie cast a quick peek at Kincaid's face. He stared at the newcomer with the glazed expression of a deer caught in oncoming headlights.

"Gloria," he said finally. "What a surprise. You went to Cancún?"

"Obviously. Why aren't you there?"

"Something came up. I had to cancel."

"I can see that. Who is this?" the woman asked, pointing disdainfully at Merrie without actually looking at her.

"Merrie Foster," he said. "She's my, er, my housekeeper's sister. She's helping out."

"I can see that." This time Gloria gave Merrie a thorough inspection that missed nothing...from the skimpy condition of her shorts to the open neck of the man's shirt tied under her breasts. "Why is she wearing your clothing? Is that a fringe benefit, or just part of the 'help'?'' she asked, snide insinuation in her voice.

An edge of anger bit into Merrie's stomach. Maybe she didn't have a working knowledge of high fashion, but she knew when she'd been insulted. Gloria had better watch herself, or she'd be flatter than burned cake.

"Gloria...please," Kincaid said in a weary tone. "This is my concern, not yours."

"It's all right, we can tell her," Merrie assured. A vaguely alarmed expression filled his eyes. "I lost my T-shirt in the tree house, and Logan was afraid it would shock the neighbors if I came down in the nude. Isn't that right?"

He didn't say anything, so she prodded his knee with her foot. "I...yeah," he muttered.

Gloria didn't appreciate the explanation. Her lips got impossibly thinner and her eyes turned a glittering blue. "Tell me, Logan...just how did she lose her little *T*-shirt?" She made *T-shirt* sound like pasties and a G-string.

"I'm not invisible. You can talk to me," Merrie snapped. "Somebody should teach you some manners. I've known two-year-olds who act nicer."

"Logan? Are you going to let your...your *maid* talk to me that way?"

"You're on your own," he drawled. "I don't have any control over Merrie. She's a free agent. And she isn't my maid."

"Darned right," Merrie shot back.

Gloria visibly squared her shoulders. "Never mind. It's just as well, I hate it when you wear such old clothing. You look like a street person. That shirt—it was dreadful. And those jeans! How can you dress that way? If you have to use casual attire, at least do it with some style."

Style? Merrie almost choked. Logan Kincaid looked better than a raspberry snow cone on a hot summer day. He'd turned her normally controlled hormones into jumping jacks. Was the woman blind, or just plain stupid?

"I dress the way I want," Kincaid growled.

Gloria waved her hand in a coolly dismissing motion. "I'm sure you could use the company expense account for appropriate purchases...or for anything you want. Father intends to pay *all* the expenses of your vacation. You're so valuable to the office, we don't want you getting burned-out."

Merrie smothered a laugh and Gloria gave her a drop-dead invitation with her eyes.

Logan briefly contemplated strangling Gloria. She had all the subtlety of a pile driver. If haughty condescension didn't work, she'd use bribery. *Damnation.* He'd escorted her to precisely three parties—social functions connected to her father's brokerage firm. Now she expected his nose in a ring...a wedding ring.

He'd sooner marry a porcupine.

Gloria was colder than an arctic night. He didn't want to get married *ever,* least of all to an iceberg.

"I can't talk right now," Logan said, deciding against strangulation. It might be a little drastic, no matter how much provocation he'd been given. "We'll chat when I get back to the office."

"Chat?" Gloria echoed incredulously.

"Miss Foster needs some medical attention." Logan gave Merrie a pleading glance. He didn't expect her to understand, but he needed help, even from such an unlikely source. She uttered a convincing groan, amusement dancing in her eyes. "Uh, I hope it isn't serious. We may have to go to the hospital."

"I'm sure she'll be fine," Gloria sputtered.

"No." He shook his head. "You can't be too careful with these things. Thanks for stopping by. Too bad we didn't run in to each other in Cancún. What a coincidence, both of us choosing the same place for a vacation. Merrie?"

He held out his hand and Merrie continued her performance, rising to her feet between heartfelt moans. He finally lifted her in his arms and hurried inside, kicking the door closed behind them. For an endless minute he waited, listening for the soft roar of Gloria's sports car. When the sound of the engine faded into the distance he breathed a sigh of relief.

"You can put me down now."

Logan grinned at Merrie. She was a mess. Her long, cinnamon hair spilled freely across them both. She had a smudge of dirt on one cheek. Her bare thighs were nestled snugly against his arms and chest. And while it was too large for her tiny frame, his shirt barely covered the most interesting portions of her anatomy...portions he'd already seen to great advantage.

"Gosh, you were in so much agony, I didn't think you could walk."

"I can walk. I can also kick."

"That's reassuring." Logan shifted Merrie so he wouldn't have such a tantalizing view. It didn't help. Putting her down might help, but he was enjoying himself too much.

Feature by feature, Merrie Foster wasn't actually beautiful. Yet as a whole? Big green eyes dominated her face. She had a stubborn little chin. And her creamy, porcelain clear skin was highlighted by masses of cinnamon hair. She'd rate a second look in any crowd.

And a third and a fourth.

"By the way," he murmured. "Thanks for rescuing me."

"It's only fair," she said. "You got me out of the tree."

"That was easy compared to Gloria Scott. You see, she's decided to get married."

"To you?"

His head rested against the glass pane of the door. "Unfortunately. I've tried to be polite. I've tried to be direct. I've tried being downright rude. But nothing seems to work. I kept my travel plans secret and she found out anyway. So I canceled my flight, blew a hotel reservation and here I am."

She wrinkled her nose at him. "Just ignore her. This isn't the Victorian age—they don't do shotgun weddings anymore."

"Ignore her?" Logan repeated incredulously. "Nobody ignores Gloria. She's exhausting; like a mosquito whining in your ear all night long. Most of the time I wouldn't care that much, but I need a vacation. A quiet, relaxing month on a beach. Nothing but sun and sleep."

"Tell her you're already married," Merrie suggested. "Or just say you have an incurable disease."

He raised one eyebrow. "Such as?"

"Terminal bachelorhood."

"That's not a lot of help."

She wiggled and he reluctantly set her on the floor. He didn't understand himself. Merrie Foster might be attractive, but she was just the sort of explosive, outspoken, impossible woman he made a point of avoiding. "Uh, come upstairs. I'll put some iodine on that scratch."

"It's fine."

"Naw. I can tell—you desperately need medical attention."

"I'm not cleaning that bathroom again," Merrie warned as she followed him up the staircase. "But I still have to finish the vacuuming. I had a little trouble with your machine."

Since Logan took the pristine state of his home for granted, the first sight of the hallway left him speechless. "Trouble" was right. Somehow the lid of the vacuum had blown off, spewing the contents in a wide arc. He grimaced as his shoes crunched grit into the polished hardwood floor.

"I take it you're not mechanically inclined?" he murmured.

"I'm okay. But that vacuum cleaner isn't just any machine," Merrie said, "it's vicious. You should get an old-fashioned sweeper, not one of those high-tech marvels. I bet you paid over two thousand dollars for that piece of junk."

He sighed.

"Anyway, like I said, it really isn't my fault."

"I know." Logan pushed her down on a stool in the bathroom. "If I'd gone on vacation, you wouldn't have burned that cake, or blown up my vacuum cleaner, or gotten stuck up a tree. Gee, I'm beginning to feel like pond scum."

Merrie surveyed him critically. "No, you're uptight and a compulsive overachiever, but I doubt if you're pond scum." She pulled the shirt up to reveal her injured back. "And Lianne says you're generous with pay and bonuses and stuff. That's kind of nice. Of course, I don't really know you, so I can't be sure."

The supple curve of Merrie's body as she leaned over triggered a gut reaction, stronger than he'd felt in a long time.

Careful, Kincaid...remember, opposites attract.

The reminder hammered in his brain as he fumbled in the medicine cabinet. Opposites might attract, but that didn't make them compatible. His parents were on opposite ends of the spectrum and had made themselves miserable, along with everyone else in their lives.

With a wry twist to his mouth, Logan pulled out the first-aid supplies. His childhood was a sore subject. He'd never forgotten the embarrassment of being the poorest kid in school, or of having the police break up fights between his mother and father because the neighbors complained about the noise.

"This'll hurt," he murmured, dabbing the nasty scratch on Merrie's spine with a cotton ball dampened in disinfectant.

"Yeow!" she shrieked.

God, he hoped she wouldn't start crying. He awkwardly patted her shoulder. "Sorry. I'll take you to the hospital if you want."

Merrie hugged her knees tighter and shook her head. "Not me. I'm tough."

"Yeah, I could tell by the way you screamed."

"Screaming helps. It hurts less that way. Can't you take a little noise?" Merrie turned her face and blinked. The only thing she could see was Logan Kincaid's belt buckle...and the area *below* the buckle. *Impressive.* Who said you could have too much of a good thing?

"Noise I can take. I'm not sure about you," he said bluntly.

"That's a fine thing to say—especially after I started thinking you weren't so bad."

"You really think I'm all right?" he asked, sounding pleased.

"I'm still forming an opinion."

Actually she was trying to assert rational thought over

renegade hormones. Sure, the man was sexy. But he still had that stupid "wife" list. She could see it from the corner of her eye—a healthy reminder that sex appeal alone did not make him a candidate for a relationship.

"I don't understand," she said abruptly, sitting upright. "Gloria seems to meet your specifications for a woman. What's the big deal?"

He frowned. "What do you mean?"

"Your list." She pointed to the roughly scribbled sheet of paper hanging from the mirror. "You know, that's a dumb way to look for a woman. You can't order traits in a person like you're ordering a hamburger."

"I'm not looking for a woman," Kincaid said, a touch of annoyance in his voice. "The list was my brother's idea. He just got over a nasty divorce, so he wanted me to think twice before I got involved with anyone. The truth is, I'm never getting married." He tossed the soiled cotton in the wastebasket and reached for some more.

"Never? That seems pretty final."

"Believe me, it's final." His expression left her in no doubt about his feelings. "Marriage doesn't work in my family. If we're smart, we avoid it completely. If we're not smart, we're miserable."

"Oh." Merrie thought for a second. "I don't know, Gloria still seems perfect, and she's rich, too. She'd be a great asset for you."

A peculiar expression crossed Kincaid's face. "Thanks a lot, but I want to make my own fortune, not marry into it," he snapped.

Whoops.

Her toes curled into the plush rug. "I wasn't trying to insult you," she murmured. "It's just that you and Gloria seem to have a lot in common according to your dumb list."

"Well, we don't." He put a bottle of hydrogen peroxide down on the counter with a thump. "And the list isn't dumb. I mean, it wouldn't be dumb if I actually wanted a wife. Compatibility is important. Aren't there certain qualities you want in a husband?"

She shrugged. "A few."

"Such as?"

Merrie gave him another examination, wishing her nerves would stop jumping—it would be a lot easier to think clearly. And it would help if Kincaid would put on a shirt. She'd seen men in various stages of undress, but none of them had done such drastic things to her breathing.

If she did have a husband list, she'd put "not too sexy" on it. She certainly didn't want a husband who embodied the perfect genetic specimen of feminine fantasies. No one needed that kind of stress.

Merrie cleared her throat. "I don't want someone who'll die of hypertension before he's fifty because he thinks money is the ultimate achievement in life."

"What's wrong with money?"

"Nothing." Merrie tossed her head. "I'm reasonably fond of the stuff myself, but you can't curl up with a bank account at night."

"Hmm. What else?"

"I want to buy my grandfather's ranch someday, so it would help if my husband wanted the same thing."

"See? You have a list, too, only it isn't written down."

He sounded so triumphant she glared.

"No, I don't see. You've got all kinds of things on that list that are particular and picky and just plain silly. Good hostess…" She started ticking items off on her fingers. "Someone who's tall, blond, reserved, elegant, composed, sophisticated…in short, you want Gloria What's-Her-Name.''

"I don't want Gloria," he repeated emphatically. "I never did."

"Then why did you date her?" Merrie asked.

"I escorted her to some office functions. That's all."

"Hmm."

"Trust me. I never get involved with a woman who has wedding rings in her eyes. Fun and casual is all I want from a relationship."

He looked so serious that Merrie bit her tongue and counted to ten. Okay. So the dope didn't want to get married. So what? Her problem was a lack of a social life. If she'd been dating like a normal woman she wouldn't have thought he was half so sexy. That was the problem with having a plan. She was scared silly she'd fall for a guy who didn't want to live on her ranch.

Get that…*her* ranch. Like she'd ever convince her grandfather to let a woman take it over. She'd only been trying to convince him since she was a kid, and she wasn't any closer to owning the Bar Nothing Ranch than she'd been at the horse-crazy age of ten.

The corners of her mouth turned down. Everyone kept saying she had to compromise—she couldn't have it all. And if she held out for the ranch before getting married, she might end up with neither.

"Why so serious?"

"Nothing," she mumbled.

"Sure. Tell me about your family's ranch."

Startled, Merrie looked at him. He couldn't read her mind, could he? "It's great. My mother is an only child, so Grandpa doesn't have a son to give it to. Of course, that's an archaic attitude, but he says he's too old to join the twentieth century and that he wouldn't want to, anyway. He keeps hoping one of my brothers will be interested in running the ranch, but I'm the only one who really cares—Cody and Daniel aren't the ranching type.''

''What about Lianne?''

''She'd rather be boiled in oil.''

Merrie rested her elbow on her knee, watching as he methodically laid out a pad of gauze, then cut strips of adhesive tape.

''So it's you, Lianne, Cody and Daniel?''

''Yup. Mom wanted to go for five, but Dad said enough was enough after Lianne was born.''

The grim set to Kincaid's mouth suggested that even *one* baby was one too many, and that four must indicate mental instability. She frowned.

''Does your grandfather want to retire?''

''Sometimes. He talks about selling the ranch so he and Grandma can move someplace warm, especially during the winter. Montana gets pretty cold.''

''I'll bet.'' Kincaid dabbed fresh disinfectant on the scratch and then blew across her skin to take the sting away. Merrie buried her face again, trying not to think about the pleasant masculine scent rolling from his body. An eternity later he finished bandaging the injury.

''All done,'' he announced.

''I suppose you want your shirt back,'' she said, sitting up and moaning. They'd hit the floor of the tree house with a bang, and despite her assurances of being tough, it had been over eight months since she'd ridden a horse or worked hard in a physical sense.

''Would you hit me if I said yes?''

''Most likely.''

''Then you'd better keep it.'' He gently tugged the shirt over the bandage and smiled. Merrie bit her lip hard enough to draw blood.

Drat. Drat. Triple drat. She didn't want to feel something for him. Sensual meltdown from a smile didn't mean anything. Not really. It was just because her thirtieth birthday was coming, reminding her about the biological clock. Men could father babies at any age, but a woman had to have a schedule if she wanted a family. And she really wanted children—three at the very least.

"Forget about the vacuuming," he murmured. "I'll get someone to take care of the house."

Merrie stiffened. It was a good thing she hadn't started trusting Kincaid. He'd probably been nice to make sure she didn't file a lawsuit for getting injured on his property.

"No way," she said stubbornly. "Lianne is a great housekeeper. You're not replacing her because of me."

"I'm not replacing anyone. I just said—"

"No." Merrie rubbed the side of her neck, thinking furiously. All at once a devilish idea struck her. "I know, you can come to Montana for your vacation. That's the answer to both our problems. It might not be a fancy resort on a sunny beach, but dude ranches are all the rage right now. It's trendy to get dirty."

"Getting dirty isn't a problem, but I—"

"It's okay," she assured. "Grandfather won't mind. The more the merrier."

"I'm sure he won't," Kincaid said, exasperated.

Merrie grinned, thinking of all the ways a down-and-dirty holiday at the ranch could knock some holes in Logan Kincaid's arrogant attitude. It might be fun—not that she'd let him get hurt. Wranglers prevented tenderfooted guests from ending up on the wrong side of a horse, or a bull.

She'd make sure a good wrangler was assigned to look out for him…it just couldn't be *her*. It wouldn't be smart to expose herself to an excess of Logan Kincaid. He could make a woman's heart do funny, stupid things. So she'd keep her distance and they'd both have a great time. After all, sleeping on a beach sounded boring. A waste of a perfectly good vacation. He needed to be saved from himself.

"It's expensive," she said cheerfully. "But I'm sure you can afford it. I usually drive to Montana, only we'd better fly to save time. A friend of mine is a travel agent—I'll call her and get two tickets to Rapid City. That's in South Dakota, but it's the nearest commercial airport to the ranch."

"I know where Rapid—"

"We can probably leave tomorrow if we hurry. It'll be great," Merrie enthused. "You'll love it. And I'm sure Grandfather will give you a discount, especially if you stay for the month."

Logan shook his head. He'd grown up in the cattle country of eastern Washington. He'd even worked at a feedlot for a couple of summers, earning money for college. It was a long time ago, but he didn't have any illusions about cattle drives and the romance of the Old West.

He bent forward, fixing Merrie with his eyes. She was impetuous and completely unsuitable. She made a prudent man want to run in the other direction...which just went to prove he wasn't prudent, because he also wanted to bury his fingers in her wild hair and taste her impudent mouth.

"I'm not interested in going to a ranch," he said, far less emphatically than he'd intended. "And certainly not for a month."

"No?" The tip of her tongue flicked across her lips and along the glistening edge of her teeth.

"No." His firmness was spoiled by the beginnings of a smile, and Logan groaned silently. He could swear Merrie didn't have any idea how tempting she was, sitting in his bathroom with her short-shorts and rumpled hair. That hair…he shook his head. It was long and loose, and would look fabulous spread across a man's pillow in the morning.

Except it wasn't possible.

The Fosters were clearly an old-fashioned family, with close ties and relationships he couldn't begin to comprehend. Merrie's sister was a creative woman who thought only of babies and a husband. Merrie might dream of owning the family ranch, but she had "forever" written all over her delicious little body…forever as in *marriage.*

If there was one thing he knew, Logan Kincaid wasn't a forever kind of guy. His notion of a long-term relationship was including nightcaps after dinner.

Schmuck.

Logan rubbed the back of his neck. From a certain point of view, his attitude didn't read so great. But it wasn't as though he pretended something different. The women he dated shared his aversion to marriage. Gloria Scott was just a fluke—she didn't count.

"Hey, are you catatonic?" Merrie waved her fingers in front of his face, one eyebrow lifted.

He shook his head. "Just thinking."

"About Gloria?" she asked, her face bright with amusement.

"Sort of. The next few weeks are going to be tough. I feel like a trophy she's trying to win. 'No' isn't in the woman's vocabulary."

Merrie wiggled on the stool, her breasts swaying against the fabric of her borrowed shirt. The tips peaked against the light abrasion and Logan shifted uncomfortably with the sudden, tight fit of his jeans.

"She's really that persistent?"

He shoved the medicinal supplies back into the cabinet. "You have no idea. I may have to move to New York sooner than expected if things get too tense. It's awkward since Gloria's father owns the firm."

Merrie fidgeted with the ends of the knot tied beneath her breasts. "You're moving to New York?"

"Sooner or later. I grew up in a small town and hated it. I prefer big cities."

She made a disgusted sound. "Seattle isn't big enough? Seattle is *huge.* We've got espresso stands on every corner and professional baseball, what else could a bona fide city lover want?"

Logan shrugged. "I want to work on Wall Street. It's the pinnacle in my kind of career."

"Boy, sounds exciting. You certainly know how to live. Traffic, noise, pollution—just wonderful." Merrie's voice was flat; she obviously didn't think much of Wall Street and New York. "So, are you really going to make a billion dollars before you're forty?"

"Not much danger of that." Logan leaned against the edge of the sink and crossed his arms over his chest. "But I'm making progress. I'm a good stockbroker."

"Who needs a vacation..." Merrie laced her fingers and stretched her arms over her head. It did intriguing things to her body and Logan narrowed his eyes.

"I told you, I'm not going to Montana."

"I know what you said. But on the other hand, would you rather stay here in Washington and wait for Gloria What's-Her-Name to come back and nag you about marriage?"

Logan stared at Merrie for a long minute, confused

emotions racing through his head. Dismay, amusement…desire. She had a drastic effect on him—an effect
bordering on pure anarchy. Gloria Scott was just annoying, but Merrie Foster could do serious damage to his
peace of mind.

Still, she was right about Gloria—the lady was nothing
if not tenacious. No one could force him into getting
married, but he might have to quit the firm if things got
too unpleasant. Besides, he *really* needed a vacation.

He'd been distracted lately. Bored. Hell, he might as
well admit he'd gotten disgusted with his wealthy clients.
They were irritating. They wanted to get richer, then
whined because they failed to follow sound advice. Time-
off was definitely a good idea. And it wouldn't be easy
to get reservations anywhere decent, not at this late date.

"What will it be?" she asked. "Orange blossoms or
horses?"

He looked at Merrie, with her eyes filled with laughter…and made up his mind. "Horses. I'll start packing."

Chapter Three

"How often do you do this?"

Merrie glanced at Logan Kincaid, sitting next to her in the small Cessna. He'd stared ahead with his jaw and fingers clenched during the entire flight. It was hard not to take his jitters personally. He obviously didn't have a lot of confidence in female pilots...or at least in *this* female pilot. From the moment they'd gotten to the private airstrip in Rapid City he'd been full of excuses why they *shouldn't* fly the second leg to the ranch.

"Do what?" She adjusted a dial and pretended to be confused by the blinking lights on the instrument panel. The plane was registered to the ranch, but she was the only member of the family with a pilot's license, so it was available whenever she wanted.

"Fly," he muttered. Logan peered out the window and Merrie waggled the wings out of pure irritation. He took one look at her hostile expression and made an obvious effort to relax.

"Once in a while," she said, intentionally sounding

vague. "But it's an expensive hobby, and I've been saving my money."

"Uh...yeah. To buy the ranch. A teacher doesn't earn that much. Saving must be hard."

The observation surprised Merrie, because she hadn't thought he'd actually listened during their conversation about marriage lists and husbands and wives, and dreams for the future.

"You'd be surprised," Merrie murmured. "I tutor students at night and I don't pay rent because I live in an apartment over my mom and dad's garage. And I earn a lot every summer working as a wrangler. I'm hoping my grandfather will be impressed by a big down payment."

Logan shifted in the cramped seat. "How did you learn to fly?"

Her mouth tightened in disgust. "It was Granddad's idea. He paid for the lessons, hoping I'd forget about wanting the ranch. He sure doesn't know much about women. But he got his money's worth, because there are a lot of tourists who don't want to drive from Rapid City. They pay well, and that way we have the plane for emergencies."

Logan shifted again, banging his elbow on the cockpit door. Merrie hid a smile; the compact Cessna wasn't designed for a man with such long legs and broad shoulders.

"Was that before or after he assigned you to the cookhouse?"

"After. Granddad had got a little more subtle by the time I turned eighteen. He graduated from blustery commands to bribery. It didn't work, but I took the lessons because I could see how handy they'd be out here."

The radio crackled and Merrie exchanged a few words with a ham operator. Seeing the familiar landmarks, she turned into the approach for the private airfield on the Bar Nothing Ranch. Kincaid tensed again as they descended and she rolled her eyes.

"I'm very good," she said pointedly. "Even Granddad flies with me."

"I'm sure you are."

"Huh. Do you want to circle the ranch to see it, or go straight in?"

"Straight in. Er...down."

"Tough guy," Merrie muttered. The wheels touched down and she taxied to a comfortable spot near a waiting pickup. A cowboy sat slouched in the driver's side, his hat tipped over his eyes. Probably Chip Packwood—he could sleep through anything. "We're here," she said unnecessarily.

"Yeah." Secretly impressed, Logan glanced around at the rolling, tree-studded hills, all golden in the long rays of afternoon light. The small airfield was meticulously maintained. On one side stood a fuel tank next to a sturdy building, with Bar Nothing Ranch lettered neatly on its side. However chauvinistic, Merrie's grandfather seemed to be a fine manager.

"You haven't said much," Merrie said, flicking switches and unfastening her belt.

He glanced back at her and shook his head. "I've been catching my breath. You're sort of like a tidal wave. I haven't had a peaceful moment in the past twenty-four hours."

Her green eyes flashed with irritation. "You didn't have to come."

The corner of his mouth twitched. He didn't want to admit he'd enjoyed being caught up in Merrie's headlong rush. He had the feeling she swept everyone along with her enthusiasm. The students she taught. Ranch guests. *Everyone*. In her own unique way, she was irresistible.

Uh-oh.

Logan took a deep breath. Irresistible wasn't a good word to attach to a woman, especially Merrie. Irresistible suggested acceptance and commitment. Even if he wanted to get married, it wouldn't be to someone so intense. Still...it might be interesting getting to know her.

"I'm here now, so I may as well make the best of things," he said casually. "How do I get the door open?"

"It's easy, like this." Merrie leaned across him and felt for the latch on the door. Logan immediately put his hand on her waist and grinned at the startled surprise in her face.

"Nice view," he drawled, his gaze flicking over the shadowed opening of her plaid shirt. She'd undone the top few buttons after they'd left Rapid City, saying it took a while to acclimatize to the heat of Montana after rainy Seattle. "Of course, it would be even better without the shirt...I should know."

"Fink," she growled, withdrawing immediately to her own side of the plane.

"For shame, you ought to be more polite to the paying guests."

"For your information, wrangler isn't spelled *h-o-o-k-e-r*," she snapped. "And don't you forget it."

"I didn't think it was," Logan said mildly. "You're awfully touchy about sex. It makes a guy wonder...are you a virgin?"

A brief flare of color hit Merrie's cheeks. "That's ridiculous," she scoffed.

His eyes widened. He'd just been teasing, but something in the tone of her voice and the instant flush made him wonder. "Uh, how old are you?"

"Never mind that."

Logan rubbed his forehead. In her tight jeans, Merrie looked like a sexy college freshman, yet she had to be older. And if she was still a virgin…he felt embarrassed and hot and *hungry,* all at the same time. "How old, Merrie?"

"All *right.* Twenty-nine." She fidgeted with the belt snapped across her waist. "Actually I'll be thirty next week." The gloomy emphasis she placed on the word thirty made him grin.

"Hey, I'm thirty-six," he said. "It's great to be thirty. People don't treat you like a kid anymore."

"You wouldn't understand, you're a man."

Oh. Logan nodded his head. He'd heard this argument before. "Let's see…the biological clock? Aren't you about ten years too early to be stressing out about it?"

"That isn't it at all. Well…maybe a little bit," Merrie qualified. "But you don't have to worry about being too old to have babies and making a success of yourself all at the same time."

Logan had heard this one, too—how men could put off getting married and starting a family, so they couldn't understand how hard it was for a woman. "Since I don't plan on having kids, that isn't much of a problem," he remarked.

"Yeah, but you have loads of time to change your mind." Merrie chewed on her bottom lip. "It isn't turning thirty, it's not…" Her voice trailed and she smiled brightly, *determinedly.* "Never mind. Everything's going to work out. I've got a plan."

He lightly tugged a lock of her cinnamon hair. It wasn't his concern, but he felt an affinity with her. They both had big plans for the future.

"Let's see," he said. "You're twenty-nine. You want

to buy your family ranch. You want kids, which presumably includes a husband in the equation. And you're a virgin.''

''I'm not...huh.'' Merrie crossed her arms over her stomach and scowled. ''That's none of your business.''

''I think your plan needs some tinkering.'' Logan leaned closer and caressed the curve of her neck. She swatted his hand but he didn't move.

''I'm not tinkering with you, so forget it. And my virginity—or lack of it,'' she added hastily, ''is my own concern. Check out the other guests if you're that desperate. We usually have a couple of single women.''

''I'm not desperate. And how do you know I wasn't talking about something else?''

''Because men always think about sex. It's your first, last and middle thought of the day.'' Merrie shimmied away, leaning against her side of the plane and looking hopefully at the nearby truck.

Logan spared the vehicle a brief glance. The sleeping driver hadn't moved a muscle. ''No help there.''

''I could scream.''

''I don't think you will.''

''You...you arrogant jerk,'' she huffed, not looking particularly worried. ''I'll scream if I want, and Chip will beat you into a pulp. He's very protective.''

He tried not to smile. ''Chip?''

''Yeah, in the truck. You can tell by his hatband.'' She wrinkled her nose, temporarily forgetting her anger. ''He always keeps a strip of condoms beneath the band, and they make these round patterns in the leather. I guess he thinks it's sexy or something, because it's obvious what's in there even when the edges don't stick out.''

Logan hesitated. Merrie Foster was perfectly capable of pulling his leg, and this sounded like a Wild West tall story. "That's an odd place to keep something like that. Surely cowboys don't wear their hats to bed."

She shrugged, an enigmatic smile on her mouth. "Cowboys wear their hats everywhere."

"Oh." Logan didn't like the smile. "I guess ol' Chip is protective. It sounds like he's got lots of protection, except it isn't the kind an innocent young thing needs to stay innocent. If you know what I mean...?"

She blinked, then laughed. "Forget it. I'm not talking. As far as the hat goes, you'll see for yourself. This is Montana—anything can happen out here. It's a land of individuality."

"Right." Logan unlatched his door and swung it open. Time for a change of subject. A *safer* subject. "So tell me, how did you choose teaching for a career? Ranching and teaching don't seem compatible."

"No, it's perfect!" Merrie followed him out of the plane, carrying some blocks connected by ropes. "We're really isolated on the Bar Nothing, so I can do home instruction when I have my own kids. See? It works out great."

In a strange way, he had to agree. It also made sense that Merrie had never made time for having intimate male friends, though he didn't think she'd admit to the fact.

He sighed, but it was a happy sigh. For someone whose vacation plans had been ruined, he wasn't having a bad time at all. This dude ranch thing seemed to be working out better than he'd expected.

Chip the sleeping cowboy didn't stir as Merrie placed the blocks against the plane wheels, at the same time explaining the maintenance building also included a hangar area in case of bad weather. She seemed a little nervous, which he understood. He'd really pushed her with that virgin bit. After all, a lot of men would probably consider virginity an affront, or maybe even a challenge.

Now he was different.

It wasn't a challenge, though it made him curious.

Curious? his conscience screamed. Right. It made him…invigorated. Anyway, Merrie certainly didn't *seem* virginal. She was confident and self-aware, which didn't mean she wasn't innocent, but it made him wonder.

"Well, if it isn't the Red Bombshell," a lazy voice announced.

"Hey, Chip." Merrie waved.

The cowboy unfolded himself from the cab of the truck and ambled over to Merrie, lifting her into a huge bear hug. He then tipped her backward and planted a dramatic kiss on her lips, all without disturbing the hat perched on his head. Logan felt his eyes narrow.

"Glad to have ya back," Chip said when he was done. "The boss sent me out to pick you up. Who's the slicker?"

"Logan Kincaid."

"Howdy, Kincaid." The cowboy held out his hand, which Logan grabbed and slowly squeezed. They were about the same height and age, though Chip's skin had clearly been weathered by a succession of long summers and harsh winters. That wasn't all. Obvious circles were clearly visible beneath the Montanan's hat. Sure enough, the man kept a supply of condoms, right where he could always count on finding them.

Logan squeezed harder.

It wasn't a conscious decision. He just didn't enjoy thinking about that kiss Merrie had received. Not that he was jealous. Not him! But he wondered how closely Chip met her idea of the perfect husband. Their discussion about her husband specifications had been rather vague.

Let's see...

She didn't want someone who'd die of hypertension at an early age. Logan remembered that, because a subtle criticism had been included in the requirement.

She didn't want someone interested in making a lot of money, because you couldn't curl up with a bank account. Okay...he could imagine curling up with Merrie would have a few advantages over a bank account, even a huge account. Though he didn't see why the two should be mutually exclusive.

And there was the ranch.

She wanted someone who would like the ranch and want to live there with her. Which qualified Chip, all right. He was all cowboy—right down to his scuffed boots and the plug of tobacco stuffed in his cheek. Of course, Logan didn't know what kind of man appealed to her. She hadn't included any physical attributes in their discussion.

The muscles in his arm bunched as he increased the pressure of their "friendly" handshake.

"Stop it!" Merrie double punched them in the shoulder and glared until they stopped squeezing and released their clenched fingers.

"Aw, Red, don't get your tail in a spin."

"My hair isn't red, and stop behaving like an obnoxious big brother. Honestly, you all act like I'm still sixteen. Now get the luggage and let's go."

Merrie stomped toward the truck and leaned against it, arms crossed. She tapped her foot, her hair a fiery halo around her head, shimmering in the late Montana sun.

"Looks red to me," Chip mumbled, looking thoroughly cowed.

Big brother?

Sixteen?

Logan shook his head. He had news for Merrie—brothers didn't go around kissing their sisters that way, and they didn't broadcast their interest in safe—and frequent—sex on their hats.

"Well?" she called, tapping her foot harder.

The two men exchanged commiserating glances. When it came to a woman's temper, they stood together. Still—not to be outdone—Logan jostled past Chip on the way to the plane, and grabbed their luggage before the cowboy could claim any kind of priority...like saying it was his job.

Logan dropped the bags in the bed of the truck next to a bale of hay, and some of the tension in his body eased as he drew a deep breath of air into his lungs. Merrie kept glaring, but he just grinned and pushed her into the cab ahead of him. There were worse ways to spend a vacation.

Chip was already behind the wheel, looking almost asleep again. He seemed to have two conditions—lecherous or somnolent. The hat was tipped over his eyes as he steered the truck, though how he could see what direction they were going defied imagination.

The working center of the ranch was less than two miles from the airstrip, and Logan's appreciation grew as they passed over cattle grids, between neat fences and well-kept outbuildings. A sprawling house stood on a slope, shaded by cottonwoods, and overlooking the surrounding hillsides.

It was an attractive setting, the ideal picture of a self-contained ranch. The one incongruity was the tent-studded field on the opposite side from the corrals. The tents weren't fancy. Just white canvas, shelter-style units that looked practical, without providing any semblance of luxury.

All at once Merrie began waving frantically at a tall man standing in the middle of the yard. She scooted over Logan's lap and out the door before the vehicle had even stopped moving. He followed at a slower pace, attempting to quell his heated response to having her bottom slide across his thighs. The woman was impossible. He doubted she had any concept of what she'd just done to his self-control.

"Granddad!"

The white-haired giant turned and caught her in his arms.

"How've you been?" she asked, her voice muffled against his chest.

"Gettin' along. Now, is this that Kincaid fellow you told me about?" he asked, releasing her with a final squeeze. He inspected Logan with a careful eye.

"Oh..." Merrie turned. "Yes. Logan Kincaid, meet Paul Harding, my grandfather."

"Pleased to meet you, sir."

The "sir" came naturally. Paul Harding was a man who commanded respect, and judging by the stubborn line to his jaw, he shared Merrie's iron will. Stalwart and honest. This wasn't someone Logan would care to cross, because if he did, he'd probably be in the wrong.

"Hmm." They measured each other until Harding finally smiled and held out his hand with typical Western hospitality. "Welcome to the Bar Nothing Ranch."

"You've got quite an operation," Logan said. "I'm really impressed. I didn't expect anything like it."

"We're meetin' the payroll." Harding's voice sounded modest, but the gleam of pride in his eyes couldn't be hidden. "That's the important thing."

"Merrie!" A tiny woman, no bigger than Merrie herself, waved from the porch of the house before darting down the hill and enveloping her in another hug. "Lord, girl, you're a sight for sore eyes."

"Grandmother...I missed you so much."

"Us? Or the ranch?" Paul Harding asked.

"Both." Merrie wrinkled her nose and smiled fondly. She got awfully frustrated with her grandfather, but he meant the world to her. She just wished he'd realize you didn't have to be a man to love ranching, or to be good at it. Brute strength wasn't everything.

From a practical standpoint, Merrie understood the business and people end of the ranch as well as anyone. And she was willing to try new technologies, like hooking into the computer world to have online reservations and information services—it didn't do any good to have a fabulous dude ranch, if nobody ever heard of you.

"And who is this?" asked her grandmother, gesturing to Logan.

"Mr. Kincaid...the man I told you about," Merrie explained. "Logan, meet Eva Harding. She's the best cook in Montana. You can bet *she's* never burned a cake."

"How do you do, ma'am?" Logan smiled his devastating smile, and her grandmother melted.

"I'm fine, young man. I've heard about you from both my granddaughters, so it's a real treat to meet you at last. Welcome to our home. Come up to the porch for some lemonade and we'll get you settled."

"Uh, Mr. Kincaid came for a vacation," Merrie said hastily. The last thing she needed was to have him staying in the ranch house. "He wants to be treated like any other dude guest. Isn't that so, Logan?"

"Sure," Logan agreed, but his tone was doubtful.

Merrie resisted digging an elbow into his side. "I thought Spike or Chip, or maybe Carl could be assigned as his wrangler. What do you think?"

A thoughtful expression crossed her grandfather's face…the kind of expression that said he knew more was going on than met the eye. "Well, now—"

"Honey, you promised to take care of me yourself," Logan protested, sounding hurt. He put his arm around her shoulder. "My own personal wrangler. I can't get into any trouble that way."

Her jaw dropped, and she was about to protest when she saw a wink pass between the two men. She gritted her teeth. *Men.* That *Y* chromosome was dangerous. The entire sex bonded and acted stupid because of it.

"Sounds like a plan," Paul Harding said with a firm nod. "Better get him set up, Merrie-girl. We can talk later."

When the older couple was far enough away not to hear her voice, Merrie shoved Kincaid away with both hands. "Very funny."

"I thought it was."

"Honey?" she mimicked. "That's disgusting. You're not really interested in me, you just want to give me a hard time for dragging you out here."

"I wouldn't say that."

"Huh."

Logan smiled and caught the edges of Merrie's collar, drawing her closer. He'd figured out she always said, "Huh" when she didn't know what else to say. "For the record, I'm very interested."

Merrie blinked.

"Do you still want to hit me?" he murmured.

"More than ever." She tried to untangle his fingers, without much success. "I'm not interested in a short-term fling, got that, Kincaid? I've got a schedule for my life, and you're not on it."

He sighed. That was the basic problem between them.

Merrie had roots. *Deep* roots. She was bound to the land and her family, while he was a temporary kind of guy. Home didn't mean that much to him, because home had always been a place of bitter arguments. Arguments over money. Over distrust. Over wanting opposite things.

It wasn't any different for him and Merrie. He wanted New York and a high-paying career. She wanted cows and a commitment. None of that would matter, except he was incredibly attracted to her, and he'd bet she felt the same for him.

"Kincaid?" she prodded.

Logan tried to collect his scattered thoughts. "How could you possibly hope to buy this ranch?" Frustrated, he made an encompassing gesture. "I don't know anything about land values in Montana, but I know you'll never manage it on a teacher's salary, no matter how much tutoring you do on the side."

Merrie shrugged, yet a trace of uncertainty burned in her green eyes. "I'm teaching to earn the down payment. Right now I'm trying to work out a payment plan between my grandfather and the bank. I'd have an income from the ranch, and I know I could swing it if he'd just agree."

"And if he doesn't?"

Pain creased her mouth. "He keeps saying it's better if he sells to an outsider, but he has to agree to my plan. Eventually. The Bar Nothing has been in our family for over a hundred years. I don't want to lose it. I want to raise my kids here and pass it down to them."

"Hell, Merrie, this is just foolishness." Logan stepped back as she bristled with indignation. He wanted to shake some sense into her, so she wouldn't break her heart over a lousy piece of land.

Good, Kincaid. Brilliant. You're so convincing.

He gave himself a mental slap.

Treat her like a client.

Great advice. He guided his clients every day, steering them away from bad investments. Most of the time he had a better than average success rate. It took diplomacy and a clear mind, because emotion tended to cloud the issue. Merrie was just like those clients; maybe he could talk her out of this crazy idea.

Friend to friend.

After all, he really liked the Foster-Harding family. And Merrie was a breath of fresh air. An honest, desirable woman, who didn't deserve to tear herself apart, fighting for something so hopeless.

Desirable?

Okay, so it wasn't quite like friend to friend.

Logan closed his eyes for a moment, then looked at her with as much calm as he could muster. "I'm sorry. This idea about the ranch—it's nice, but you're a romantic. That's not always practical in the real world."

"Romantic?" Merrie stared incredulously.

"Aren't you?"

She shook her head in disgust. "I know all about the real world—ranching isn't romantic, it's hard work that never ends. The pay is lousy and your life is completely unpredictable. The only reason we didn't go bankrupt years ago is because tourists *think* it's romantic, so they pay big bucks to spend a week roping cattle."

"Oh." He didn't know what else to say.

He still believed Merrie was looking at the ranch with stars in her eyes. It wouldn't be hard. She'd spent all her summers in Montana, reveling in the freedom and beauty of the wild land. But owning and running a ranch on a year-round basis was a far cry from summer vacations when the weather was nice and the daily responsibility rested on someone else's shoulders.

Merrie marched toward the tent-covered hillside. Giving her a good lead, Logan followed, a wry smile creasing his mouth. Tents? Naturally. He'd canceled his reservations at the most comfortable, expensive resort in Cancún, Mexico. Now he was going to sleep in a tent.

On the ground.

And he'd bet they didn't even have air mattresses.

At the beginning of the encampment Merrie stopped and waited for him to catch up. "Grab an end," she muttered, pointing to a canvas roll.

Fatalism descended. Not only had he traded an opulent hotel for a tent, but he'd have to set it up himself. And tents weren't the most private places in the world, which made it a little difficult to have a romantic encounter. An image of Merrie, warm and willing in his sleeping bag, spun through his brain. Well…maybe they could work it out.

Moron. Idiot. Sexist jerk.

Wonderful. He could call himself every name in the world, but he couldn't stop thinking about her. Virgin or not, she appealed to him in the most basic of ways. Boy, he was stupid. He'd gone mushy over a woman he barely knew. A woman who literally wanted it all…a ranch, marriage, children. *Everything.*

With careful planning and a lot of sacrifice, he could almost see her getting the ranch. *Almost.* But he believed in practical dreaming, not building castles in the air. That was part of what had destroyed his parents' lives. Besides, she didn't trust him worth a lick. She didn't approve of his career, or his house, or anything.

So he shouldn't like Merrie Foster…yet he did. He liked her too damned much.

"Does this look good?" Merrie pointed to a clear area at the top of a small hummock.

"Sure. Let's get that tent up." Logan smiled his most charming smile. It didn't work—she had an "I'm going to be nice to the dumb tourist even if it kills me" expression on her face.

Dredging up memories of long-ago camping trips with school groups and childhood friends, he managed to assist without looking too inept. It was easier to look skilled when she dragged him to one of the barns and picked out a horse for him to ride.

"Dust Devil...this is Logan Kincaid. You're going to be friends," Merrie announced, patting the velvety nose of the animal.

"Dust Devil?"

"He's a little skittish."

"Right." Logan didn't believe her. She knew it had been a while since he'd done any riding. One thing he was certain about, Merrie wouldn't take any risks with a "tenderfoot." She prided herself on being a good wrangler.

Dust Devil snorted softly and nudged Logan's shoulder with his head, then methodically checked his pockets for any tasty morsels that might be lurking there.

"Rub his nose and let him smell you. But use a firm approach," she advised.

Logan lifted his eyebrows. "What does that do?"

"It's a matter of establishing dominance."

"I see." Grinning, Logan patted Dust Devil's neck, then ducked under the horse's black head and approached Merrie. "Dominance, huh?"

"With horses," she snapped.

"I thought it sounded too easy."

"Logan Kincaid, you're a...a..."

"Yes?" He stroked his forefinger down the curve of Merrie's cheek and let it rest in the fluttering hollow of her throat. "What deadly insult do you want to heap on my head?"

"Remember that list of yours. I don't have any of the qualifications. I'm not blond, or tall, or anything on that stupid thing."

"My brother's idea, not mine."

She inched backward until she came up against one of the stalls at the back of the barn. "That's right, you're not getting married. Ever. You don't want a wife, so that list doesn't mean anything." She sounded willing to be convinced.

"But you want a husband."

With Logan Kincaid staring at her with such blatant hunger in his face, Merrie didn't know what she wanted. She'd never considered herself particularly attractive. Nice enough looking, with an acceptable figure. But she was too short, her eyes were too big, and she had a pointed chin. Pixieish, according to one former boyfriend.

In other words, *cute*.

Cute was death to a woman's confidence. Kittens and newborn foals were cute. She wanted to be sexy. And when Logan Kincaid looked at her, she felt sexy. This definitely wasn't good, because he wasn't in her plan, and he wasn't going to change, so it didn't matter what he made her feel.

"Kincaid."

"Call me Logan." He leaned closer, filling her senses with warmth, trailing the back of his fingers across her lips. "You smell good," he whispered.

"So do you," she couldn't help saying. "But it isn't me, it's the hay. Hay always smells good."

Logan lifted her chin and smiled. "It isn't the hay, but

I'll check for sure.'' He edged even closer and put his face against her hair, inhaling deeply. ''Nope, just you. Mmm, this feels nice.''

Nice? Merrie frowned. He'd gotten her all hot and bothered, but he just felt *nice?* There wasn't any justice in the world. ''Are you going to kiss me or not?'' she demanded.

''I was thinking about it.''

''Stop thinking.'' She slid her fingers through the rough silk of his hair and pulled, at the same time knowing she wouldn't have much luck if he didn't actually want to kiss her. There was too much difference in height and strength.

Then suddenly the difference didn't matter, because her feet left solid footing and Logan Kincaid was wrapped around her. Holding, supporting…burning.

Small, gentle kisses coaxed her lips, a tingling contrast to the power of his grasp and the unyielding wood pressed against her back. Of course, she saw strong men every day at the ranch. Cowboys needed to be tough. But Logan didn't do that kind of work, so it was surprising that he would be so…she moaned when he shifted, pressing the evidence of his response against her.

Instinctively she dropped her head backward, and he rewarded her with murmuring sounds of encouragement.

Another moan welled deep in her throat and was lost in a renewed assault upon her mouth. It wasn't gentle, yet it didn't hurt. She was caught in a storm that was hot and violent and exciting, all at the same time.

''Logan…''

''Yes,'' he whispered, thrusting his tongue between her parted lips. He tasted incredible. Right. *Perfect.* And she shivered between long, slow strokes that sent streams of fire through her veins, filling her with a restless, aching need.

A faint "yee haw" in the distance barely registered, nor did the answering nicker of the horses remaining in the barn. But the snuffle of a large, equine nose in her neck restored reality in a hurry.

"Logan?"

"Mmm." His left hand moved up her rib cage.

"Logan!"

"I'm here, honey."

Exasperation dampened the turmoil still churning in her body, and she pushed his wandering fingers away. "I know you're here. But it's getting late, so in a minute a lot of other people are going to be here, too."

"What?"

Merrie wiggled until her feet touched the floor of the barn. "Everyone's coming back."

Logan turned his head and listened for a moment to the faraway noises made by a happy, tired group. He smiled. "We've got plenty of time." He cupped her face in his palms and kissed her again.

Her resolve weakened and she swayed. It was so nice, this funny, uncontrolled excitement. And it seemed inevitable. There had been an awareness between them from the beginning, something that defied understanding, but existed just the same.

All at once Merrie pulled away and stared at Logan's face. Inevitable?

"Uh-oh," she gulped, and bolted for the door.

Chapter Four

Logan caught up with her ten feet away from the barn and pulled her to a stop. "I don't think Dust Devil is the skittish one around here," he said.

Merrie crossed her arms over her stomach and lifted her chin defiantly. "Dust Devil is gelded. I don't think he's capable of getting skittish."

"Gelded?" Logan raised an eyebrow. "Rough stuff."

"And don't you forget it."

"I'm not forgetting anything." He ran his fingers through his hair. "And I'm especially not finished discussing what happened in there."

"Jeez!" Merrie choked on an exasperated shriek. According to the books about such things, men weren't talkers. They didn't discuss feelings or any of the things important to a woman, so Logan probably just wanted to know when they could have a cozy repeat. "I'll save us both some time—it's not happening again."

"The hell it isn't," he said bluntly.

Her mouth dropped open. "I'm saying no. Get it? *No*."

Logan gave her a level look. "Uh-uh. You're saying you're scared."

"Wrong." She poked her finger in his chest for emphasis. "This isn't fear, this is self-preservation. I can't afford to get mixed up with you, Logan Kincaid."

"Why not?"

"Well, for one thing you're too pretty."

He gaped at her. "Pretty? I'm a man. I'm not pretty. I'm...rugged."

Merrie bit the inside of her cheek. Pretty had been the wrong word. Logan wasn't pretty, he was perfect. Great hair, terrific body—even his smile, with the slightly uneven edge to his teeth, was perfect. Too perfect for a would-be woman rancher. He was smart and ambitious, and he wanted to live in New York and make a zillion dollars.

"Okay, you're not pretty."

"Thank you very much," he snapped, seeming equally irritated with the retraction.

Ego. She grimaced. "I just meant that you're a loner. You're champagne and expensive cars and big cities. I'm...this." Merrie gestured around the ranch complex. "I don't want to get involved with someone so different from me, because it can't come to anything."

"Damn," Logan muttered under his breath. Merrie had picked the exact argument hammering in his own head.

They were different. Opposites. As much as she attracted him, he wouldn't offer white lace and wedding rings. It wouldn't be fair to start thinking that way—he wasn't the best husband prospect. Cripes, he didn't even know how a good marriage worked.

"And you're not a bad guy, but—"

"I know this speech," he interrupted. "You're going to suggest we be friends, not lovers."

"Becoming lovers was never a possibility," she said sweetly. "And I'm not even sure about friendship."

His lips twitched. Merrie didn't give an inch. The lady had an obstinate determination that went beyond mere stubbornness. But then…maybe she was right. Maybe they shouldn't take the chance of becoming too attracted to each other. It was a good way to ruin their lives.

No.

You can handle it.

Logan sighed at the insistent, persuasive voice. Rational thinking had nothing to do with it—the voice came from a much lower place than his head…it was centered in the pit of his belly and controlled by physical need. He reached out and tugged a shimmering strand of her hair.

"An impasse?" he murmured.

"Sounds like it."

Like hell, he thought, getting annoyed. People could enjoy each other without planning to get married, as long as they were straight with each other. They just had to remember they were having a summer flirtation…no commitments or ties. It would be good for both of them—Merrie needed to relax and have fun just as much as he did. All she needed was convincing.

In the back of his mind Logan realized there was a flaw in his reasoning, but he didn't care.

Neither of them moved as riders began appearing over the hill, bringing dust and cheerful greetings. A number of them called to Merrie, welcoming her "home."

"You're on," he murmured. "Do your wrangler thing."

Merrie's gaze flicked to the approaching guests and back to Logan. "So...we understand each other?"

"Perfectly."

A hint of suspicion crept into her eyes, though he maintained his best poker face. Heck, he knew it was a great poker face—he could win a hand with nothing but a pair of deuces and the suggestion of a triumphant smile hovering on his mouth. Though it was probably that same smile getting him in trouble right now.

"Logan...you *are* going to behave? Right?"

"Don't worry." His tone dropped and he leaned closer. "I'm going to be very, very good."

"That isn't what I asked!" Merrie snapped. She set her pointed little chin and glared at him.

"But I like kissing you."

"Rat fink," she muttered. "I'm warning you, *behave.*" Giving him a final threatening look, she straightened her shirt, plastered a determined smile on her face, and waved to the approaching guests.

A rider with the lanky build of a beanpole spurred his horse into a gallop ahead of the others. "Welcome back," he said before swinging down and giving Merrie a smacking kiss.

Logan's muscles tensed.

"Wow! You're here! Mr. Harding said you wouldn't be coming for a while," a freckled youngster exclaimed as he rode up next. He jumped from his horse and grinned happily. It was obvious he had a crush on Merrie.

"Hi, Toby. Remember...you have to keep hold of your horse," she warned.

Toby hastily collected the dropped reins. "This is so great. I've been trying to convince Mom and Dad to come back later in the summer to see you—it's no fun when you're not here."

A flash of guilt nagged at Logan. The unplanned change in his vacation had affected a lot of people, including this prepubescent kid with an adult-size case of puppy love.

Merrie ruffled the youngster's hair. "I'm sure you've been having a great time without me."

"Uh-uh," Toby said earnestly. "It isn't the same."

"It sure isn't," several of the guests agreed together, and they looked at Merrie with warm affection.

"Nobody gets anything going at night. The barn dances are so dull...we just sit around staring at each other," an older woman declared. "But it'll be different now that you're here."

Logan shook his head. Evidently many of the guests returned summer after summer, so they knew Merrie quite well. She was so popular, he'd be lucky to get five minutes alone with her.

"I even learned to dance this year," Toby said. He wrinkled his nose. "Square dancing. It isn't so bad, not once you get started. It's just really—"

"Square," she finished for him.

The adults around them chuckled at the old joke and Toby shrugged sheepishly. "Yeah. It wouldn't be so bad if the calls were different—but all that dosey-dozy stuff sounds really stupid."

"That's dos-a-dos, and it isn't stupid," Merrie said. "It's traditional Old West dancing. Cowboys did it all the time."

"Hey, Red!"

Another cowpoke grabbed Merrie into a kiss and Logan's eyes narrowed to mere slits. He didn't have any right to be possessive about Merrie, but these guys were carrying Western hospitality too far. First Chip with his condom-ringed hat, then the beanpole and now *this* guy.

"Hi, Spike. Keeping out of trouble?" she asked when he finally released her.

"Gee, Red. That hurts. I'm a real sweetheart."

"I know, that's why I asked."

Spike grinned. "Babe, you know you're the only woman for me. Just say the word and we'll tie the knot."

"Knot is right...I'd sooner hang."

The cowboy pretended he was terribly wounded, then ambled away, heading for a shapely brunette who was giving him an inviting smile. Merrie didn't seem perturbed and Logan got the feeling vacation affairs were the norm, rather than the exception, on the Bar Nothing ranch.

But not for Merrie.

Nope.

She had her plan, and a city slicker wasn't part of that plan. Which definitely didn't sit well with Logan, because he was a slicker through and through, and didn't have any intention of changing that condition.

Or of getting married, either, which was also part of Merrie's blasted plan.

Logan scowled, then caught Merrie looking at him with an exasperated expression. He wanted to beat his head on the barn door. Lust wasn't a terminal condition, but he didn't want to prove that fact for himself.

He stepped closer and lifted an eyebrow. "What's the matter, *babe?* You said you wanted to get married, then you rejected that attractive proposal. I'll bet Spike wouldn't mind staying on the ranch and giving you a couple dozen children."

"Logan?"

"Hmm?"

"Shut up."

Merrie turned on her heel and stalked away from Logan Kincaid, muttering dire things about his life expectancy, ancestry and his generally bleak hope of surviving the next few days without broken bones.

Men were all the same. They didn't want you—not *really*—but they didn't want anyone else to want you, either. Not even in play. And that's all it was with the guys on the ranch...playtime. They kidded around and gave her mock kisses. They certainly didn't make her feel...well, like the kiss Logan had given her.

Merrie shoved the thought away with equal amounts of embarrassment, wonder and pure vexation. Logan's interest in her was limited—comparable to a short-term lease. Partial rights, but no permanent responsibility. He was on vacation and wanted to loosen up.

Fine.

He could loosen up with someone else.

She had bigger fish to fry.

Fish? Oh, God. She was thinking in clichés. That wasn't good. She must have been crazy to bring Logan Kincaid to Montana. He scrambled her brain—like an electric egg beater with a defenseless egg. Merrie set her jaw. This was one egg who wasn't getting beaten.

"Come on, folks, let's get these animals rubbed down," she called briskly. "Cowboys take care of their horses before anything else."

The guests groaned.

"Don't blame me. There isn't an automatic car wash in over a hundred miles. Well...at least fifty," she said.

The good-natured groans turned into laughter and everyone followed their respective wranglers. Care and feeding of the horses was an important feature of life on the Bar Nothing Ranch. The dudes were responsible for their mounts the same as anyone, though they got a lot of assistance, particularly at the beginning of their visit.

"What can I do?"

Merrie peeked at the source of her irritation. For all the world, Logan looked eager and willing to help, which she knew couldn't be true. Curry combs and sweat were a long way from a posh resort in Mexico.

"Leave me alone."

He grinned…his slow and lazy grin that turned her inside out. "Now, honey, that isn't very nice—you're my personal wrangler. You wouldn't abandon me, would you?"

She coiled a rope over her arm. "I'd like to drop you off a cliff."

Logan clucked at her. "That isn't a nice thing to say. If you're not careful, you'll shock the other guests."

"Like you'd care," Merrie muttered, at the same time glancing around to see if anyone was close enough to overhear them. "And I'm sure they'd sympathize about the cliff. They might even help."

"Shame on you." Logan hooked his thumbs in his belt loops, enjoying himself too much to heed the annoyed look in Merrie's green eyes. "Is that Western hospitality at work?"

"Now, *listen*—"

"Merrie! You're back!"

Logan glared at yet another cowboy ambling toward them. "So help me, they're everywhere," he muttered. He changed his stance, putting one hand on the fence rail and leaning subtly closer to Merrie.

The cowboy stopped cold. The two men measured each other for a long second, then the ranch hand gave Merrie a chaste kiss on the forehead. "Glad to see ya, Red."

"Likewise."

The man hastily retreated and she sighed. "Okay. What did you do?"

Logan lifted his eyebrows. "I don't know what you're talking about."

Merrie rolled her eyes. "Right. You warned him off somehow. This may be a ranch, but I'm not a cow, and no one puts a brand on me. Got it?"

The corners of his mouth lifted. "A brand, honey? You're confused. Remember me? The guy with terminal bachelorhood? I'm not interested in putting a brand on any woman. Or a cow, for that matter," he added thoughtfully.

She shoved the rope into his chest and Logan grasped it automatically. His nose wrinkled slightly, because the worn hemp had a certain distinctive aroma he remembered from his summers at the feedlot—manure.

"What should I do with this, honey?"

"Stop calling me that!"

"Sure, Red."

"Urggh!" she yelped. "My hair isn't red."

He tossed the coiled rope over a fence post and caught her arm before she could escape. "You've got cinnamon hair and a flaming temper—which naturally makes a man wonder how much other heat you keep hidden."

Merrie trembled, feeling a searing blast of the heat Logan was talking about. She was coming to the dismal realization that it wasn't self-control that had kept her focused on owning the ranch, but lack of any real temptation. Temptation like Logan Kincaid.

"That isn't any of your concern," she mumbled.

"I wouldn't say that." He rubbed his thumb across the soft skin at the base of her wrist. Her pulse quickened, skipping faster with each feathered stroke.

"Logan," she moaned. "Stop. This isn't…everyone will think we're involved."

"Aren't we?"

She opened her eyes, pleading with him. "Please don't do this. I can't get distracted."

"I think that's an insult. Don't you like me, honey?"

Merrie shrugged. "I like you. Well…sort of." She bit her lip, trying to decide how much she should admit—it could be like setting fire to dry grass. Only she'd never been good at hiding her feelings. "I'd probably like going to bed with you, but it would create all kinds of problems."

"What kinds of problems?"

Heart failure.

Bliss.

Oh…*tarnation.* She blinked at her unruly thoughts and tried to focus on something else.

"Think about it, Logan. You're good at affairs. I'm not. I don't go into anything halfway, planning to get out in a couple days. If it wasn't for Gloria What's-Her-Name, you wouldn't be in Montana at all."

Logan shifted his feet uneasily. He didn't know what would have happened if Gloria hadn't shown up, giving him an excuse to go with Merrie. And it was a damned lame excuse, too.

Hell, she's *been honest. What's wrong with you?* his conscience screamed, and it slowly worked through Logan's brain that he would have found a reason to go to Montana, even if Gloria hadn't arrived at his house at such an opportune instant. The realization sent a cold chill down his spine.

"I…" He cleared his throat.

"Exactly."

Though they had been saying and thinking different

things, the fundamental meaning was the same. Merrie was as enduring as a clear mountain lake, he was as temporary as a wave flowing across a sandy beach. Yet when he looked at her, his normally logical thinking got completely tangled.

"So," he said slowly, "what do we do?"

"For starters, let go of my hand."

Belatedly Logan realized he was still caressing Merrie's wrist, stroking the tips of his fingers across her delicate skin. "Oh...sorry."

Merrie pulled her arm back and thrust both hands into her back pockets for safekeeping. "We'll pretend we're two old friends while you're here, and when you leave, we never have to see each other again."

Logan had news for Merrie—he'd never kissed a *friend* like that, and he'd never been good at pretending. But what the hell? He was on vacation, ready for new experiences. He could always try, and getting to know Merrie would be a very intriguing activity.

"Friends," he agreed, mentally crossing his fingers, just in case. "Only you still have to be my wrangler. I'm not doing this dude ranch thing alone. You got me here, so I'm your responsibility."

Merrie regarded him for a wary minute. "Okay. But right now I have to check in with my grandparents. And...and work on tonight's entertainment. I'll see you later."

Oh, yeah. The boring barn dances that wouldn't be boring now that Merrie was here.

Logan nodded. "Sure."

He watched Merrie climb the slope to the house and nearly groaned.

Why was he doing this to himself?

For a smart guy, he was acting awfully dumb—positively begging for the worst kind of frustration. Merrie might think she was a tough ranching type, yet everything about her was womanly and inviting. She couldn't even walk up the hill in jeans and boots without letting her hips sway in unconscious provocation.

It was hard to believe that she and Lianne were sisters. Lianne was determinedly feminine, from her eyelet blouses to her calico skirts. Only he'd never felt the slightest sexual interest in her—a nice woman, that's how he thought of Lianne Foster.

But Merrie...Logan sighed. Merrie with her fiery hair and green eyes, her delectable little body—she made him burn like blue blazes. And she wasn't even a tall blonde. She was a stubborn redhead.

My hair isn't red.

He grinned reluctantly. Merrie didn't seem to mind being called "Red" when she wasn't upset, yet the nickname didn't sit well when her temper was roused. He should threaten her with a cold shower when her mouth got all stubborn and angry like that.

Thinking of which...Logan glanced toward the utilitarian facilities the Bar Nothing Ranch offered their guests. Merrie had pointed them out earlier. Very basic and unembellished. Commodes and showers, and the showers had limited hot water.

Oh, well.

He shrugged with philosophical acceptance. Trying to be friends with Merrie was going to take a lot of work and effort. He'd probably need a few cold showers before his vacation was over.

Like a few thousand.

Merrie sighed and rolled over in bed. She hadn't slept well. And as much as she'd like to blame Logan, it was

Logan lifted an eyebrow at the grizzled old man standing by the food table, a butcher's knife in one hand, and a long, two-tined fork in the other. "Is he for real, or the dude ranch version of the Hollywood trail cook? Rough and salty, but with a heart of gold?"

"For real," Merrie said, trying to stay annoyed. And failing.

It was still early, and the tent was occupied only by ranch employees. The guests would wander in over the next hour, many just for tea or coffee. Breakfast was one of the less communal meals since most people weren't accustomed to rising at dawn and eating like lumberjacks.

"Hi there, Bandit," Logan said, leaning over to ruffle the fur between the shepherd's alert ears. They'd been introduced the previous evening.

Bandit wumphed companionably, his tail swishing.

Merrie and Logan filled their plates and he nudged her to a quiet corner of the tent, away from the cordial wranglers who invited them over.

"Thanks...we're fine," he said.

The men didn't argue, though their faces were filled with curiosity. A few even snickered behind their mustaches and beards, speculation rampant in their eyes. Merrie gave them a warning glare and followed Logan. Bandit disappeared under the table, where he hoped to find scraps from plates descending in his direction.

"How was your tent?" she asked. "Warm enough?"

"It was great." He grinned over the rim of his cup. "I'm glad you care."

"I don't."

"That's a bald-faced lie." He moved his foot until his leg brushed along hers. "I'm a guest, and you care about all the guests."

"Yeah," she muttered, shifting her leg.

Logan cut a bite from his steak, seeming not to notice her retreat. "This is terrific. I didn't expect that old coot to be such a good cook."

Merrie watched Logan eat, surprised he enjoyed the simple fare. He even seemed to like the coffee, which was an even bigger surprise. Seattle had a thing about coffee. There was an espresso stand on every corner where patrons ordered things like Mocha Java Talls and Why Bothers, which were nonfat, decaf, sugar-free lattes.

Nope, it wasn't just coffee in Seattle. It was a religion, and a far cry from the rough buckaroo brew served at the Bar Nothing.

"Are all the meals like this?"

She blinked. "Pretty much. We're a ranch, and people expect generous portions. But I insisted we add some of the lighter stuff, like fruit and bagels. Along with some vegetarian choices in the other meals."

"How did the cook take that?"

"Not well." Merrie laughed. "Harvey never heard of low-fat cooking. And it's a lot easier to turn a side of beef on the barbecue and stir a pot of chili than worry about such 'fancy notions.'"

Harvey might have disagreed with Merrie's decision, but Logan didn't need to see the evidence to know who had won the battle. What Merrie lacked in size, she made up for in sheer grit. Which was puzzling, considering her grandfather's reluctance to trust her with the Bar Nothing. "I take it Harvey *doesn't* have a secret heart of gold?"

A wry smile creased her mouth. "Maybe. *Somewhere.* Actually he didn't start out as a cook. He worked cattle until his bum leg got too bad. He's had some hard times, so I guess his attitude is understandable."

Logan studied Harvey as he argued with one of the

ranch hands about whether his steak had been rare enough. The weathered cook finally turned, speared a raw slab of beef sitting next to the grill and slapped it on the other man's plate.

"That rare enough for you, sonny?" Harvey bellowed.

"Uh..."

A wave of the butcher knife apparently decided the matter.

"It's just fine." Defeated, the ranch hand slunk back to his table, amidst the general teasing of his companions.

"Hmm," Logan murmured. "I don't think he's in danger of winning any prizes for charm."

Merrie laughed. "No, though he doesn't pull that stuff with the paying guests—he's too loyal. You see, Harvey lost his own spread in the seventies...a combination of bad weather and crashing beef prices. Granddad gave him a job and he's been here ever since."

"Your grandfather seems like a great guy."

Her smile softened. Merrie obviously loved Paul Harding, even if he threatened to prevent her dream...the dream she wanted more than anything else in the world. "Granddad believes in three basic rules—tell the truth, help your neighbor and keep your promises."

"That about covers things."

"Yeah. There isn't any other way to survive out here."

She rested her chin in her hand, a faraway expression in her green eyes, and Logan stopped eating. Merrie was such an odd mixture—one minute as bright and energetic as a field of poppies waving in the sun, and in the next she glowed with mystery and magic.

"Ranch life isn't so different now than it was a hundred years ago," she murmured. "We have modern conveniences and technology, but none of them make a bit of difference when the temperature drops and a blizzard is blowing. Then it's just you and Mother Nature, fighting to see who wins.''

He leaned forward. ''I thought you only spent summers in Montana.''

''Not always.'' Merrie shook her head. ''I lived here the year after I graduated from college. It was one of the worst winters on record. Of course—'' she chuckled ''—Granddad hoped it would discourage me.''

''But it didn't.'' Logan's statement wasn't a question. He didn't think mere blizzards would discourage Merrie Foster. She was made of far sterner stuff than anything Mother Nature could throw at her.

''Nope,'' she agreed cheerfully. ''I love taking care of animals and protecting them. There's something wonderful about being connected to the land. Fundamental. That's part of the appeal of dude ranches. It's so... uncomplicated.''

That almost made Logan laugh. There was nothing uncomplicated about Merrie. She might think she was basic and down to earth, but that only made her harder to figure out.

''You'd better finish your breakfast,'' Merrie said, taking a last bite of her fruit and getting up. Despite the hearty fare offered, Logan noticed she'd eaten lightly. ''Granddad assigned us to throw a circle around the northwest end of the ranch, so it'll be a long day.''

He hated to admit his ignorance, but it wouldn't do any good to pretend he knew what she was talking about. ''Throw a circle?''

''Oh...yeah.'' Merrie looked a little startled that he didn't understand, and Logan took it as a compliment. ''We have to move the cattle in that section to better grazing. Grandmother is packing us a lunch. We're the only riders going that direction, so we won't be anywhere near the chuck wagon.''

Logan glanced at Harvey, who was standing over his gas-fired grill, muttering to himself. ''I guess there are all kinds of advantages to the arrangement.''

She smiled faintly. ''Say that again when you wake up tomorrow. Eight hours in the saddle isn't the best first day you could have.''

''I'll survive.''

''No doubt,'' she muttered, an unexpected grimace on her lips.

''Hey, what did I do?''

''Nothing. I'll meet you at the barn in twenty minutes. We'll saddle the horses and get going.''

Merrie turned, and Logan watched as she walked away, Bandit appearing instantly at her heels. She stopped to tease the bleary-eyed guests who were filtering in for breakfast. She already knew the newcomer's names, and had a special greeting for each of the returning ''dudes.''

Logan's business instincts didn't know he was on vacation—they immediately clicked into gear. It took more than cattle savvy to make a dude ranch successful. Merrie had explained the typical stay at the Bar Nothing was Tuesday through Saturday night, and that stay didn't come cheap. Folks might come once, lured by a set of well-chosen words in an advertisement, but they'd never return if they didn't enjoy themselves to the hilt.

Merrie made sure everyone had fun. Yet somehow, he thought it had less to do with her being a good businesswoman, and more to do with her being an intrinsically friendly person.

Absently Logan took a swallow from his cup and

winced as the dregs yielded a scattering of coffee grounds.

"Put her down."

Startled, he looked into the glowering face of Harvey, who proceeded to slosh a stream of hot black liquid into his cup. Coffee splattered across the table and a pool of it rolled along a crease in the red-checked, plastic tablecloth.

"Er, thanks."

The old man waved the battered coffeepot in his face. "Don't you do nothin' to hurt her, boy. I'm watchin' ya." A fierce scowl punctuated the warning.

An unbidden smile curved Logan's mouth. The identity of "her" was unmistakable—it seemed Harvey's missing heart of gold rested squarely in Merrie's small hands. "Don't worry."

The old man uttered an explicit word. "I was young once, too, and I seen t'way ya look at her. Ain't no city buck with his brains in his pants gonna do somethin' to our Merrie-girl."

Logan whistled under his breath. He hadn't thought his feelings for Merrie were so conspicuous. Damn, he should have realized it would be obvious to anyone with a suspicious mind. Particularly a suspicious fellow *male* mind.

"I'm not planning to hurt her."

"Mind you don't." The cook stomped away, his hard life evident from his game leg and bony frame. Tattered but not beaten, the old fellow still possessed a basic dignity.

Logan shook his head and dug into his cooling breakfast. If he didn't meet Merrie in the specified twenty minutes, she'd probably ride out without him. And Logan intended for them to spend every possible moment together. It wasn't smart, but he hadn't been able to stop thinking about Merrie since finding her in his tree.

Now that would make a great story for the grandchildren.

Logan's arm froze, his coffee cup lifted halfway to his mouth. His brain was completely out of control. Hell, for that matter, Harvey was right. His brains *were* in his pants.

He glanced at the evil brew in his cup. Maybe if it was strong enough it would knock some sense into him.

Chapter Five

This is the life.

Logan took a deep breath and grinned at nothing in particular. Everything seemed perfect, from the blue sky above, to the sway and creak of the saddle as Dust Devil stepped along the summit of a hill. Leaning over, he patted the horse's sleek black neck.

Despite his ominous name, Dust Devil was an amiable, well-mannered mount. He'd quickly accepted a new rider, and he had an easy gait, comfortable for someone who hadn't ridden in a long while.

In the distance, Bandit raced down gullies and up slopes, occasionally appearing to frisk around the horses, his mouth open in a big canine smile.

"This is terrific," Logan said quietly, looking at Merrie.

She was riding beside him, her eyes half closed, her face raised to the sunshine, as though it was pouring through her in a living river of gold. Her loosely braided hair allowed wisps and curls to escape, framing her face with fire, while a cowboy hat hung down her back.

Oh, Merrie, Logan sighed to himself, caught somewhere between appreciation and pain.

She was so beautiful. Her body swayed with the horse beneath her, moving as one with the huge animal. Yet there was nothing careless about Merrie's control over the palomino. Her fingers held the reins with the skill of a born rider, alert to the slightest change of direction or temper.

"I can't believe I resisted coming to Montana," Logan confessed. "I was sure wrong. It's a great place for a vacation."

Merrie opened her eyes and smiled lazily. "The great Logan Kincaid wrong?"

"I never said I was great."

Her lips twitched. "Yeah?"

"Certainly not. I may have implied we'd be great together in bed, but that's completely different."

"I thought we buried that subject."

"Not as deep as I'd like to," Logan said significantly.

Faint color burned in Merrie's cheeks, and he grinned. Nobody who grew up working a ranch could be ignorant of the basic facts of life, yet she still seemed innocent in so many ways.

"Just friends, Logan. Remember?"

"I remember."

I remember being awake till three in the morning and deciding friendship is for the birds.

It was rather underhanded, planning a campaign of sensual persuasion while pretending to be friends. But she'd just go prickly again and start preaching about the differences between them. Hell, he knew all about the differences. Nobody had to paint a picture for him—getting involved with Merrie was just asking for trouble.

Yet Logan couldn't help himself…even with warnings from knife-wielding ornery cooks and his own instincts for self-preservation yelling for attention.

"So, what does everyone do on the Bar Nothing, besides throwing a circle?"

"Oh…" Merrie shrugged. "Ranch work is unpredictable, but there are regular tasks that have to be planned. The guests do almost everything, though some jobs are less popular than others." She gave him a sideways glance, filled with wicked amusement. "The week we castrate and brand the calves, for example. Want to come back next spring for that?"

"No. You have an evil sense of humor," Logan complained, though it was without heat. "Castration isn't anything to joke about."

"Feeling a little threatened, are we?"

"Not a chance."

"Tough guy, huh?"

Clucking to her mount, Merrie cantered in front of him. Dust Devil pricked his ears forward, yet aside from that, he showed no interest in following the other horse.

They had been riding for several hours over the rolling hills, rising gradually in elevation. When they reached the northernmost point of their "circle," they would sweep back in, moving the cattle they found to fresh grazing. From what Merrie had already explained, he knew a large part of working the herd consisted of moving cattle from one place to another, to make certain they got proper feed and didn't destroy the plant cycle.

Which reminded him…the best way to get Merrie to open up was to talk about the ranch.

"Hey, Merrie?" Logan called. "Did your family ever

get involved in the wars between sheepherders and cattlemen?''

Up ahead, Merrie tightened her fingers on the reins. Sun Spot snorted, resenting the brief restraint. He was more spirited than the mounts used by the dudes—an excellent cutting horse, but not overly complacent.

''Easy, boy,'' she soothed, and Sun Spot tossed his silvery-gold head as though he understood. ''You had a nice gallop this morning, and it's getting too hot to race right now.''

A long run would have suited Merrie, too. She wanted to get far away from Logan Kincaid. It was the smartest thing she could do, except it was her responsibility as a wrangler to take care of him. Though...it didn't seem Logan needed taking care of—he'd saddled Dust Devil without help and mounted the horse as easily as though he'd been doing it every day.

Naturally.

Logan did everything well.

She turned and watched him ride closer. His face was relaxed, with none of the anxiety most of the dudes exhibited for the first day or two. His summers working a feedlot must have been more educational than he'd let her think.

''What was that about sheep?'' she asked.

''I just wondered if the Hardings got involved in the range wars,'' he answered. ''Weren't things pretty violent back then? All that Wild West stuff?''

''Wild West? Let's see...'' Merrie said thoughtfully. ''According to Granddad, my great-great-uncle was killed in a crooked poker game out behind the old barn.''

Logan grinned his mind-numbing grin. ''I'll bet that didn't have anything to do with sheep.''

''Not unless one of them had an ace up its fleece. Uncle Ezra didn't tolerate cheating. Unfortunately he was also a heavy drinker and a lousy shot.''

''Oops...bad combination.''

''You said it.'' Merrie blew a strand of hair from her damp forehead, then lifted her hat over her head to block the growing heat of the sun. ''As for the battle between sheep and cattle, a lot of the early ranchers were involved at one time or another.''

''Was it that serious?''

She lifted one eyebrow. ''Of course it was. They had open-range grazing, and sheep do more damage to the range than cattle. Sheep also paid off a lot of mortgages because they're more profitable.''

''Does the Bar Noth—''

''Nope. No sheep,'' Merrie said, anticipating the question. ''Not ever. I'm not sure, but it's probably written into my great-grandfather's will that any descendant who brought a woolie on his land would be struck down by lightning.''

Logan reached over and tugged the braid hanging over her shoulder. ''A man of conviction.''

''We're fighters,'' she warned, yet her voice held a wry acceptance. Logan's sensual advances seemed inevitable. And breathtaking. It had never been that way with a man before. While she'd dated a few guys, she'd never really gotten involved. Most men were put off by her dream of owning the ranch—they didn't think it was feminine or something.

Only Logan didn't seem to care. It wasn't that he wanted to live on the ranch or marry her...he just wanted to make love. With her.

Simple, unadorned desire.

Last night her grandmother had called it a compliment, one of the most honest compliments a man ever paid a woman. Of course, she'd also said that didn't mean the woman had to go along.

Blast.

Grandmother was practical and down-to-earth. But Grandmother wasn't sitting in Merrie's shoes being tempted by the sexiest man in Montana *or* Seattle.

"Merrie? You seem a million miles away. Is everything all right?" Logan sounded genuinely concerned and she shook her head.

"I'm fine. If you're ready for lunch, we can eat up there." Merrie pointed to a lofty outcropping.

A few minutes later they tied their horses to a tree and Merrie walked to the edge. The land fell away in a sea of hills...an endless pattern of gold and green, spiked by cottonwoods and pines and rock. Yet it was all dwarfed by the vastness of the sky.

And nowhere, in any direction, could you see the impact of "civilization." Merrie often thought this was exactly how the first settlers had seen Montana, and why they'd named it big sky country.

"I love it here," she murmured. "It's the highest point on the ranch. And the most beautiful."

Logan looked out across the landscape and saw a hawk in the distance, wheeling through the blue expanse, proclaiming its freedom. The wild cry sank into him, and the tight knot of tension in his body eased more than he'd thought possible. The demands of clients, the rise and fall of stock prices and the need to prove himself, seemed far away.

"What do you think, Logan?"

He turned. "You're right, it's beautiful."

A pleased smile curved her lips. "I don't usually bring visitors here. It's special to me."

The shy admission made Logan feel ten feet tall. Merrie had shared her private, special place with him. "I'm honored. You could have taken me the long way around."

"I did. How do you think we got here?"

He laughed and helped as she inspected their picnic site for sunning rattlesnakes, then spread a blanket in the shade beneath a tree and pulled their food from the saddlebags. A light breeze ruffled the grass, enough to keep them cool.

Bandit instantly appeared to claim his own lunch, settling a few feet away with his dog chow, the bowl of water Merrie poured for him and a meaty bone.

As they ate, Merrie talked about the ranch and its history. She had a tolerant humor for the various types of people who had visited over the years, and a clear understanding of what it took to make a dude ranch successful.

Logan was impressed. More than impressed. For all her scatterbrained, outlandish behavior, she might be able to run the place successfully.

"Where do we ride from here?" he asked when the last sandwich and brownie had been eaten. The combination of food and sun and fresh air was making him drowsy. It wasn't surprising, considering how little he'd slept the previous night.

"We start circling at this point," Merrie said lazily. She was lying on the blanket, hands tucked behind her head and her eyes closed. "We'll ride the fence line to make sure it's intact, then come down a little valley on the northwest side of this ridge."

Logan rested on one elbow next to her. Nice. Very nice. The top of her shirt was unbuttoned, exposing the shadowed valley between her breasts. Somehow, he doubted she was aware that he could see the lacy fabric of her bra...or the faint outline of a dusky nipple.

"Uh, how important is moving the cattle today?"

She opened her eyes. "Cowboys don't take naps, if that's what you're asking."

"I'm not the one lying down."

Merrie's eyelids drifted down again. "Just letting the food settle."

"That doesn't answer my question. What about moving the cattle?"

"Hmm." She arched her neck with languid grace. "Grandfather is matchmaking. The cattle are fine up here for another week."

If it had been any other woman lying there, the candid admission would have sent chills of foreboding up Logan's spine. But as much as Merrie wanted to get married, she plainly didn't want to marry *him*. Paul Harding could matchmake all he liked, and nothing would come of it because his granddaughter wasn't interested in a big city stockbroker. Which should have delighted the stockbroker in question, though somehow it didn't.

"I see. What gave him that idea...about matchmaking?"

"You did, with all those 'honeys' and pleas for 'my own personal wrangler,'" she growled disgustedly. "What did you expect him to think?"

With the tip of his finger, Logan traced the intricate twists of her auburn braid. "If it was my granddaughter, I wouldn't trust me within a mile of you."

"You have to have children before getting grandchildren, so I don't think you have anything to worry about. Besides, he doesn't trust you...he trusts me," Merrie said dryly.

"And I thought he was a smart man."

"He is, but to quote a cliché, 'hope springs eternal.' You're the latest volley in a campaign to make me forget the ranch...or to find someone to run it with me. Actually that's run it *for* me. Grandfather doesn't have a clue about women—the Bar Nothing would have sunk a long time ago without my grandmother." Though her words were tart, her tone was laced with resigned amusement.

A faint frown tightened Logan's mouth. Paul Harding didn't strike him as a fool—he had some old-fashioned attitudes perhaps, but he definitely wasn't a fool. He had to see that Merrie was a big reason the Bar Nothing was so popular. "Maybe he has his own reasons for not selling you the ranch. Reasons he isn't telling you."

Merrie lifted her head and looked at him with guarded eyes. "Such as?"

"I don't know." Logan shrugged. "Maybe he doesn't want you to break your heart on this place."

She settled down again. "Selling the family ranch to a stranger would break my heart a lot faster."

Logan watched her a moment longer, then glanced out at the magnificent view. Bandit lay with his muzzle on his forelegs, already asleep, yet clearly responsive to the odors and sounds carried to him on the breeze. They wouldn't have to worry about snakes if they took a nap as well—either Bandit or the horses would alert them of any problems.

Except Logan didn't want to sleep. Merrie's unique scent made him achingly aware of his own maleness—a heavy, throbbing heat that hadn't completely vanished since he'd first seen her.

He touched her hair again. "It seems expensive to assign a personal wrangler to each dude," he murmured.

For a long moment she didn't answer, and he thought

she'd drifted asleep. "Not everyone gets a personal wrangler," she said finally.

"Oh? I'm flattered."

She made a sound that might have been a laugh. "Sometimes it's a one-on-one assignment, and other times a wrangler is assigned to a group of two or three. It depends on the level of riding experience."

"Experience, eh? So much for flattery."

"Huh."

The gentle rise and fall of Merrie's chest as she breathed threatened to burn Logan alive. He'd seen her in the green shadows of the tree house, full and taut with lush promise. More than anything, he wanted to trace the lacy bra...then slip his fingers beneath to cup her breasts and feel her nipples harden in response to his touch. He wanted to see her clothed only in sunlight and the warmth of his breath.

Her voice brought him back to reality. "I'll bet you could even be a wrangler if you wanted," she mumbled drowsily. "You're a natural rider."

"It really isn't one of my life's goals."

"You don't have to remind me—cowboys don't make a lot of money. They never have."

"Still...even if they don't get paid a lot, it seems expensive to hire so many wranglers."

"So is staying at the Bar Nothing." Merrie yawned and rolled over to face him. "Logan, it could only happen in America. I *told* you...people have this romantic notion of cattle ranching and are willing to pay for a chance to be part of it—even if it's only for a week. Where else could you charge someone two hundred and fifty bucks a day to sleep in a tent and get worked like a dog?"

"And you even make them set up the tent," he drawled.

"Of course. Naturally children get a discount. We only charge a hundred and fifty if they're under fourteen, and nothing for the under age five crowd. Not that we get many really young kids, since there isn't a lot they can do here."

He chuckled softly. "Come to think of it, I never asked about my discount."

"You can afford it."

Could he? Logan wasn't worried about the money, but a much bigger cost—the damage to his peace of mind. Merrie made him take every good intention he'd ever formed and toss it to the wind. She was dangerous.

"Honey, about that *friend* stuff...?"

Her face got suspicious. "What about it?"

"It isn't going to work."

"Sure it is. You're in a terrific place, with lots of good food and fresh air. What do you need sex for?"

His jaw dropped. She couldn't be serious, could she? He sneaked a peak at her earnest green eyes and shook his head. Darned if she wasn't.

"I can't pretend to be friends."

"We agreed—"

"I don't care what we agreed," he said, frustrated. "I was going to try to keep things neutral like you wanted, only I couldn't stop thinking about you. Then I decided to be sneaky—to pretend to go along and still try to seduce you, but I can't, dammit. You aren't the kind of woman a man sneaks around."

"Well, you can't seduce me, either!"

"Don't make a bet on it."

She glared and set her chin, and it occurred to him that she was right. *Seduce* was the wrong word. Merrie might be relatively innocent, but she wasn't a woman easily swayed. Anything she did would be of her own free choice.

"Okay. I can't seduce you," he agreed. "But think about it…an uncomplicated, hot affair might be just what you need." Logan's tone lowered. "And it would be hot. I promise."

"Sorry. I'm not into one-night stands."

His breath hissed out harshly. "That's not what I'm talking about."

Her eyes were sad and wistful at the same time, and he could see the battle waging between her mind and her body. "Whether it lasted a month or six months, it would still be a one-night stand," she whispered.

"It wouldn't be like that." Logan wasn't sure what he was protesting. On a gut level, he knew making love to her would be unique. Special. Something he'd always treasure. "Please, honey, give it a chance. You're attracted to me, I know you are. And you've been working so hard to get this ranch, you've forgotten how to have fun. So have I. We can teach each other to relax."

The muscles in her throat worked as she swallowed fiercely. "You don't know what you're asking."

"I…" He stopped. Maybe he didn't. Men and women looked at sex in different ways. For one thing, he had to admit that men were a lot less discriminating.

Hell.

Logan's eyes widened as a new thought struck him— he didn't actually know what any woman looked for in a relationship. It was possible he really *didn't* have anything to offer Merrie beyond a hot affair. The thought was…disturbing.

"Why does it have to be all or nothing with you?" he asked, his voice edged with desperation. He'd never wanted anything so much as he wanted Merrie. She was so different from the women he knew—no calculation in her eyes, just a baffling honesty and single-minded determination.

"I can't change the way I am." Merrie bit the inside of her mouth as she watched Logan stare back at her.

Was she crazy?

A woman could spend her entire life without meeting a man like Logan Kincaid, much less have him desire her with such intensity. On top of which, he didn't act all conceited—a lot of men with his looks and money would be impossible.

Merrie reached out and touched the crisp lock of brown hair falling over his forehead.

"I guess we're not that different in some ways," she murmured, unable to keep from scooting closer. He was warm and strong, and she ached with a hunger that food couldn't satisfy.

"Yeah?"

"Yeah. You're right. We've been working so hard we've both forgotten to have fun. Not that I'm saying we should have an affair," Merrie added hastily.

"Of course not."

She touched the tiny laugh lines bracketing Logan's mouth and the strong curve of his chin, telling herself it was just curiosity. After all, she didn't *need* to touch him. *Liar.*

Merrie sighed. She wasn't good at self-deception. Her body clamored for the kind of embrace he'd given her in the barn...shoulder to shoulder, hip to hip, infused with blatant intimacy. There had to be a way of fixing things.

"We could help each other," she said huskily. "I mean, as friends and stuff."

"Uh, sure. Friends are important."

His eyes had a glazed look and Merrie felt a secret

surge of triumph. "And friends kiss sometimes. It doesn't have to go further than that."

"God…" he groaned, sliding his hand around her nape. "You're making me crazy."

"Tit for tat," she whispered.

Muttering something about half a loaf, Logan fastened his lips over hers. In the back of Merrie's mind she'd expected it to be calmer this time. Not so passionate. A simple kiss to ease the tension…sort of like drinking a Bloody Mary to cure a hangover.

She hadn't thought the ache could get worse.

It did, and the realization was as frightening as the power Logan seemed to have over her body. Yet she didn't want it to end, and she dropped her head, inviting a deeper caress. In answer, he thrust his tongue between her teeth and stroked the inner softness he found.

Velvet to velvet, fire to fire.

Of their own accord, Merrie's fingers explored Logan's arms and back, memorizing the hard shape of him. Learning each muscle, bunching and releasing as he moved. She'd never forget this moment, taken out of time and space, and provoking her with a soul-burning passion.

"Pure honey," Logan breathed into her mouth.

"No, just brownies," Merrie managed to sass between his gliding forays. "A touch of chocolate aphrodisiac."

He lifted over her slightly, his broad shoulders silhouetted against the tree and sky above them. "I don't need any chocolate…or anything else to tempt me."

Merrie shifted restlessly, driven by the tense need that licked her senses. It was magic…warmth pouring from the sun, the purity of Montana air, and this man who made her feel more than she'd ever felt in her life.

"Logan," she whispered, "what am I going to do with you?"

"I'd probably shock you with any suggestions."

His white teeth gleamed in a smile, a sharp contrast to his tanned skin, and she wondered where he'd gotten his sun-bronzed color. She couldn't see Logan using a tanning booth at the local gym—he might be almost perfect, but he wasn't vain.

"How can a stockbroker get so tanned?" she murmured.

"Corner office with a window. Isn't success great?"

She punched him lightly in the ribs and he chuckled. "Actually I do most of my own yard work. And I run whenever I have time—I don't like treadmills, so that leaves the great outdoors."

That explained why he was so strong. There were several acres on his property—composed of both woodland and landscaped garden, requiring a lot of effort. Running and working outdoors were an incongruous match to a stockbroker, but nothing about Logan was especially logical.

"No gardener, huh?"

"Nope."

"I thought all wealthy people had gardeners. It's kind of a status symbol."

A pained expression crossed his face. "I know you don't believe me, but money is just a scorecard, Merrie. That's all. And I enjoy hard work, so why pay someone else to do it for me?"

"I guess."

Logan called money a scorecard, but his life seemed to be built around that scorecard. It really wasn't her concern. She'd already interfered enough, dragging him to the ranch. Maybe he would have been better off sleeping on a beach and being bored. Still...he was so different from what she'd expected. So much more alive and vital. It seemed such a waste for him to spend his life closed-up in an office.

Lifting her hand, she traced the strong contours of his face, the dark eyebrows, sculpted cheekbones…his sensual mouth. Without seeming to move, he caught her finger between his lips and sucked for an instant.

Heat rolled through Merrie, melting her into the blanket and the earth beneath. What would Logan say if he knew his sexy asides and hints didn't shock her as much as he thought? Oh, they made her hot and uncomfortable inside, but it had little to do with embarrassment.

"May…maybe this isn't such a good idea," she whispered as he kissed her again…long, drugging kisses that didn't seem to begin or end, so much as sweep over her like the tumbling currents of an ceaseless ocean wave.

"It's a hell of an idea," he muttered.

Half hell. Half heaven, Logan thought to himself, and he groaned into her sweet mouth. He hadn't expected to touch her again, not so soon. Merrie Foster had an iron will. It was no surprise that her ancestors had been early settlers, carving a home from the wild land. They'd passed on their stubborn determination…the spirit and will never to quit.

He tugged at the end of her braid, then began separating the long strands from their confinement. Some devil or instinct made him want to see Merrie surrounded by the shimmering layers of her hair, as though she'd just wakened in his bed.

She was everything and more than he'd dreamed about in the past two days. Her skin, delicately flushed with sultry warmth. Her eyes…heavy-lidded and darkened to a lustrous malachite. Her hair in all its bright glory, spread across the blanket and grass.

Without conscious thought, he'd unbuttoned her shirt

to her waist, and now he brushed the cloth away from the feminine bounty it framed, more than concealed.

"No..." Merrie protested, shaking like an aspen leaf in the wind. "We agreed...just a kiss."

"Just a kiss," he repeated, dipping down to kiss the flushed crown of her left breast. "Sweet...so damned sweet," he muttered, gliding his tongue across the lace-covered mound and prompting a broken cry from her throat.

Merrie was so responsive, it seemed impossible she could be inexperienced. He knew she wanted him. She moved in concert with his body, touching as much as she was touched. Demanding the same response that he demanded. Matched perfectly.

Logan undid the front clasp of the bra and thrust it aside.

"L...Logan?" she said hoarsely.

"I'm here," he breathed, drawing the velvety hardness of her nipple into his mouth, while his fingers played with the other, tugging gently at the rigid peak. It was all he could do to keep from dragging the zipper of her jeans down...to discover the hidden warmth between her legs.

"Logan...no." Merrie pushed his shoulders with surprising strength and he groaned.

"Honey..."

"*No.*" The stormy, unhappy note to her voice sliced him in two. "We have to stop."

Logan groaned again, his body arched in frustration. But it was Merrie's choice. *Wholly.*

He rolled away and stared at the rugged landscape. Here he was, stuck on a ranch with a woman who turned him on harder and faster than any woman he'd ever met before. A forever kind of woman who just wanted to be friends.

How had he gotten himself in such a mess?

Chapter Six

Logan rolled over in his sleeping bag and stared at the canvas tent above him. He'd been on the ranch for six days. Six of the most frustrating...and best days of his life. Damned if he wasn't having more fun than he'd ever thought possible.

Merrie was a pint-size tornado who swept everyone along in her path. The drawbacks of lukewarm showers and a hard ground to sleep on seemed insignificant when she laughed and teased her way through the day.

Her grandparents loved her dearly.

The guests adored her.

All the cowboys were wild about her—they'd crawl naked through a field of cockleburs if she asked them.

And Logan was dying of frustration, even when she made him laugh—which she did a lot. There hadn't been any more kisses, "friendly" or not. Mostly it was tough, dirty work. In his unique position of being a long-term visitor and "friend of the family," he got drafted into all kinds of chores, which weren't part of the usual vacation package.

Like haying.

Or shoveling manure from horse stalls.

All of which was still fun, because Merrie attacked every task with the same exuberance she applied to working cattle or riding fence lines.

Logan had asked Eva Harding about paying for his visit, only to be brushed off with an indulgent smile. Hell, he'd happily pay the full price as long as Merrie stayed next to him, with her bright laughter...and the shimmering awareness in her green eyes. That was the only thing keeping him sane—the knowledge that Merrie wanted him as much as he wanted her.

Yawning, Logan crawled out into the cool morning. The sun still sat below the horizon, though the stars had begun to fade from the sky. He stretched, then hiked toward the showers with a towel-wrapped bundle under his arm. It was Wednesday morning, the first morning with a new group of "dudes." While they might not have realized the iffy possibility of hot water, it was better to arrive early than take his chances.

"Good morning." The husky contralto of Merrie's voice came from the shadows around the low building.

His body tightened with pleasure. "Good morning."

She held out a box. "Grandmother washed your clothing. I was going to put them by your tent, but since you're already awake...here you go."

He peered inside, seeing his shirts, jeans and other garments neatly folded within. "Gee, I think she likes me."

"I can't imagine why," Merrie retorted. "You being such a stuffed shirt and all."

Logan's mouth twisted ironically, though he knew Merrie only meant to tease him. Truthfully he *was* uncomfortable around the Hardings. It wasn't their fault. Families...*happy* families were a mystery to him, and he'd often seen Merrie watching him with a puzzled frown on her face when he couldn't relax in their welcoming circle.

Perhaps it was better that way.

As much as he desired Merrie, they didn't have much common ground. She belonged on the ranch and he was headed back to the city after his vacation.

Damn. Logan didn't want to think about leaving. Not yet. They had plenty of time left. His immediate future with Merrie was the only thing he wanted to think about.

"How about taking a shower with a stuffed shirt?" he drawled. "I'll scrub your back...and anything else that might need washing."

She turned toward the house. "Not a chance."

"I didn't think so, but I had to ask...friend."

Merrie bit on her lip to keep from smiling. Logan didn't give up...he just varied his tactics. "I'll see you at breakfast," she said over her shoulder. "Be sure to bring an appetite."

Behind her, Logan muttered something vaguely lecherous, having to do with appetites and what really made him hungry. Merrie just kept walking.

If anyone had predicted she'd enjoy spending time with Logan Kincaid, she would have said they were crazy. He was a stockbroker, for heaven's sake. Just the name of his career was enough to raise images of peevish, antacid guzzling men with "hypertension" and "early death" tattooed across their foreheads. At least, that's what she'd always thought.

But Logan didn't talk about investments or stock portfolios, though he seemed interested in her ideas for the ranch. Mostly, the only "stock" he talked about were horses and cattle. And he worked hard, turning his hand to the dirtiest, most unglamorous jobs.

"Is everything all right, dear?" her grandmother asked as she drifted into the kitchen, a pensive look on her face.

Merrie looked up. "Sure. What could be wrong?"

"I don't know...something connected to your young man, I suppose."

"He isn't my young man." But she bit the inside of her lip, staring at the vase of wildflowers on the table. "Logan just wants to, uh, fool around."

"That could be nice."

"Eva Harding, that isn't a proper thing for a grandmother to say," Merrie scolded. "You're supposed to be worried about my virtue, not encouraging me to do something foolish."

"Virtue is such an old-fashioned word," Eva said complacently. "I prefer to think of it as exploring your possibilities."

"There aren't any possibilities. Logan is interested in sex. Period. He certainly isn't in love with me."

The elder woman's smile was serene. "Don't let that bother you. Men tend to think with their bodies first...it takes a while for their hearts to catch up. But eventually they do."

Merrie's own heart skipped a couple of beats. "No, it's not like that. I mean, I don't *want* him to fall in love with me. He'd never want to live on the ranch."

"The Bar Nothing isn't everything, darling."

"Don't say that." Merrie crossed her arms over her uneasy stomach. "You don't agree with Granddad, do you? That I can't handle the ranch because I'm a woman?"

Eva shook her head, though her eyes were troubled. "No, dear. I know you could do it. But it would be a lot easier with a man like Logan. Don't give up on him, dear. He's a good man and he may surprise you."

Give up on him? Merrie winced. Nothing could come of her friendship with Logan, no matter what her grandmother thought. He'd made it very clear he wasn't interested in a permanent relationship—either in Seattle, New York *or* Montana. Besides, even if he wanted to get married, she didn't meet any of the basic qualifications on his silly "wife" list.

And she didn't care, anyway.

Right?

Absolutely. Merrie looked out the front window, seeing the beauty of the open land falling away. This was home. Logan might make her heart pound and turn her palms damp, but that's where it ended. The idea of them falling in love was ludicrous...so ludicrous she grinned at the thought.

When all else failed, she could rely on her sense of humor.

Merrie felt almost calm when she walked into the mess tent an hour later. Logan sat at one of the tables, joking with the other cowboys...he got along fine with them so long as they didn't try to kiss her.

If he'd been any other man she'd suspect him of being jealous, but jealousy and male possessiveness weren't quite the same thing. Logan had simply staked out his claim, and didn't want any poachers before he'd played it out.

Merrie's eyes narrowed, but Logan just waved, motioning to the empty chair across from him. She crossed her arms stubbornly and stayed put.

"Hey, Red," said a voice in her ear. "You got a burr under your saddle?"

She glanced at Chip. He'd restocked the condoms under his hatband, having depleted the supply the previous week with a lady CEO from Los Angeles. One thing about Chip, he made no promises and was honest about his intentions—heck, he advertised them on his hat.

"I'm fine."

"Sure you are, Red." Chip rolled a handmade cigarette and stuck it in his shirt pocket for later enjoyment—they didn't allow smoking in the mess tent. "You know what? I kind of like Logan. He isn't bad for a slicker."

"Men always stick together," she muttered direly.

"Now, Red."

"I'm going to eat."

The cowboys chatting with Logan scattered as she walked up and plunked her plate down, tipping their hats and making up dumb excuses why they had to leave.

"What did you do?" Merrie asked wryly. "Threaten them with tar and feathers if we weren't left alone?"

"Nonsense. I'm a very civilized sort of guy." Logan assumed a wounded expression as he took a swallow of coffee. "Don't you enjoy having breakfast with me?"

She ducked her head to hide her amusement, at the same time slipping a piece of bacon to Bandit. "You've charmed everyone else on the ranch, why worry about me?"

"But, honey, you're my personal—"

"—wrangler," she finished for him. "That excuse is wearing thin. You need a wrangler like I need a hole in the head."

"You promised."

"Huh."

He grinned his devastating best, and she forgot why she was annoyed. Men like that shouldn't be allowed around women, they could make them do all sorts of silly things—like forget their own name.

The visitors drifted slowly into the tent, lured by the smells of coffee and the cinnamon rolls Eva Harding always baked the first morning a fresh group slept at the Bar Nothing. Merrie got up and joined her grandparents, who were chatting with the different families.

New visitors always had lots of questions about the ranch and what they'd be doing. Kids were the most fun. They threw themselves into being "cowboys" without a self-conscious thought. By the time they left, most would be talking with a Western drawl and riding circles around their more reticent parents.

Merrie smiled, pushing aside the vague yearning Logan always made her feel. Logan Kincaid could be a friend, not a lover. After all, owning the Bar Nothing would be a lot more satisfying than a temporary relationship with an uptight stockbroker who despised marriage.

At least, that's what she kept telling herself.

Logan sat and drank more coffee while he waited for Merrie. He loved watching her in action. She just plain liked people, and it showed.

After a while everyone began gravitating toward the main barn, where they would be matched with mounts and wranglers, and discreetly observed for their level of ability.

"You'll love it," Merrie enthused to a shy teenage boy. "There's nothing like sitting on a good cutting horse and moving the herd. I'll bet you're great with horses."

The boy looked at her with adoring eyes and Logan shook his head. Another conquest.

Despite the noise and bustle of unskilled "hands," the horses stood patiently, accepting timid pats on the nose and the laborious process of being saddled. And through it all, Merrie darted in and out, encouraging and making them all feel at home.

But later…Logan's eyes gleamed in anticipation, they'd ride alone, and he might make some progress. Merrie had to be getting tired of this "friend" business.

Then all at once, a piercing, *demanding* voice cut across the happy bustle.

"My God, Logan. *This* is where you've been hiding? In this…this *place?*"

He looked up and saw Gloria Scott standing ten feet away from him, dressed in designer silk and the hand-made, leather Italian pumps she prattled about constantly. The pumps had suffered a bit—they weren't intended for walking through a barnyard. His mouth twitched.

"Hi, Gloria. Nice to see you."

"Ugh. You're…you're *filthy.*"

Logan glanced down at his jeans where he had brushed a streak of dust from his hands, then shrugged and leaned against the corral fence. "What brings you to Montana?"

Gloria's icy blue eyes got colder. "We didn't know where you'd gone. Father was concerned…he's called and called your answering machine."

"Sorry…I forgot to check for messages." Logan tried not to laugh, but it was difficult. Why had he let Gloria's marriage schemes annoy him so much? She was a riot— he should have been laughing all this time rather than wasting energy gritting his teeth.

"Logan?" Merrie said at his elbow.

He glanced down and put a lazy arm around her shoulder. "Hi, honey. Guess who dropped in?"

Gloria's face was remarkably similar to a cat whose tail has been shut in a door. "How charming. You went on vacation with your maid. Logan, dear, that's very democratic, but I don't think it was the best idea."

Merrie dropped the bridle she'd been carrying...possibly to free her arms for action. "Now see here, you don't have any—"

"Honey...she's a guest," Logan said hastily, tightening his hold on Merrie. She looked ready to beat the other woman into the ground with a broom handle. And while he'd enjoy watching, he'd rather have Merrie expend her energy in a more rewarding direction...like with him.

"I'm not anybody's maid."

"Of course not," he soothed, then looked at Gloria and gave her a totally innocent smile. "Merrie's family owns the Bar Nothing ranch. It's quite a place—they offer the finest dude vacations in the country."

Gloria didn't look impressed.

Then a truly wicked idea occurred to Logan. "I'm awfully glad to see you. You can be the first to congratulate us...Merrie and I are getting married." Without dropping a beat, he put his other arm around Merrie's waist, pulled her close and kissed her astonished mouth.

A startled murmur rippled through the crowded yard, evidence they'd heard his announcement. Whispers of "Did you hear that?" and "How romantic" were mixed with an outraged scream from Gloria.

Married?

Furious, Merrie pushed at Logan's chest without success. The miserable rat—he was just having fun at her expense. Still...she couldn't keep from moaning at the heat of his open kiss.

It wasn't wise to get near him. She was too vulnerable...her body too responsive to his warmth and strength. Casual sex and quickie affairs might appeal to Logan Kincaid, but she wasn't made that way. Since that afternoon on the ridge, she hadn't let him touch her any more than necessary.

As soon as she was free, she'd throw Logan to the wolves. Actually one wolf…Gloria What's-Her-Name and her insulting, snobbish attitude. They deserved each other. She'd rescued him from the woman once already, that's all he could reasonably expect in a single lifetime.

Yet when Logan's grip loosened, Merrie couldn't help clinging to his shirt. Her knees felt funny—sort of like they belonged to a newborn calf.

"I'll get you for this," she whispered, gulping several breaths of air. She peeked to one side and saw an array of faces, staring at them with shades of delight, excitement and confusion.

Except for Gloria. Gloria looked like the Wicked Witch of the West after she'd been doused with water. A perfect, freeze-frame pickle face.

Oh, well. Merrie shrugged mentally. It wouldn't hurt to play along. Her "engagement" could last a few minutes, and she'd tell everyone the truth after Gloria left.

"We were supposed to tell my family first, *darling*," she told Logan sweetly. "We agreed to keep it a secret until then."

"I couldn't help myself, honey." He kissed the corner of her mouth with a foolishly adoring expression on his face. "I wanted to share the news with my old friend. And I know how you feel about friends. Isn't that right, sweetheart?"

The "friend" part almost got him kicked, but Merrie remembered at the last moment that it wouldn't seem very affectionate for a new fiancée.

"Right, darling," she said, at the same time trying to unclench her jaw.

All the endearments were beginning to nauseate her, and they weren't doing much for Gloria, either. Though she still seemed a little green, a calculating look had crept into the woman's eyes.

"This is so sudden, Logan," Gloria drawled.

"It came as a surprise to me, too," he said cheerfully. "You know how I feel about marriage."

"Yes, of course. But your little Merrie, er, what was the name?"

"Foster," Merrie supplied, returning Gloria's synthetic smile with one of her own.

"Miss *Foster* seems to have changed your mind about getting married."

"You bet. There's nothing like taking a relaxing vacation together—it really gets you close. I fully recommend it if you want to get married."

Merrie bit her lip. Logan was terrible. He was deliberately rubbing Gloria's nose in the fact that she'd ruined his vacation plans in Mexico—only to have her husband "quarry" caught by someone else in Montana. Even if the other woman suspected their engagement was bogus, it couldn't be pleasant.

Gloria squared her shoulders. "I see. You're right, I'd like to stay for one of these dude vacations and see what happens. You have room for me, don't you, *Miss* Foster?"

"Er..." Merrie gulped imperceptibly, aware of everyone's avid gaze upon them. Forget the romance of the West, they were enthralled with the immediate drama of a lovers' triangle. Even the wranglers were leaning closer, waiting to hear what would happen next.

"We always have room for one more," she mumbled.

"That's right." Logan gently pulled her close, so that her back rested against his chest. He crossed his arms over her breasts, and though it was ridiculous, he was warm and solid and made her feel protected. "Honey, I have an idea...how about assigning Chip as Miss Scott's wrangler?"

Merrie choked and Logan kissed her hair, whispering a suggestion that she control herself...while his body shook with suppressed laughter.

"How about it, Chip?" he asked, lifting his head. "You free to handle this for us?"

Chip ambled forward. "Be happy to take care of the little lady. Don't you worry about nothin', ma'am," he said, tipping his hat to Gloria before spitting a stream of tobacco juice into the corral. "We'll get you all taken care of."

Gloria's eyes had widened to an impossible degree. Chip was the antithesis of a wealthy urban dweller—from his faded jeans and ancient cowboy boots, to the infamous rings beneath his hatband.

"I do *not* think—"

"You're sure lucky he's available," Logan assured her smoothly. "Chip is one of the best wranglers at the Bar Nothing. Not as good as Merrie, of course, but you'll be fine."

"I...yes," Merrie said briskly, breaking free of Logan's embrace. "Let's go everyone, it's time to get mounted up. We have cattle to move."

She didn't risk looking at Logan for fear of giggling. The man was impossible...though with all things considered, Chip and Gloria probably belonged with each other. If nothing else, they'd keep the crowd entertained.

Reluctantly the dudes and wranglers sorted themselves out, then rode away, many with wistful, backward glances. They didn't want to miss anything, particularly any fireworks that might occur.

Chip shooed Gloria toward her car, telling her to change into something that a horse wouldn't take insult to…and that if she didn't have anything, then he and the "boys" would rustle something up. With a last, fulminating glare that encompassed Chip, Merrie, and especially Logan, she flounced to the dust-covered sports car.

"Can you handle that?" Merrie asked.

"Don't worry, Red," Chip said, unperturbed. "I've tangled with more than one wildcat. Got the scars to prove it, too." He grinned and ambled in Gloria's direction.

"I'll put fifty on Chip," Logan murmured into Merrie's ear.

She made a disgusted sound. "I can't believe I let you do that to me. Engaged? What will my grandparents think?"

"That you have excellent taste?"

Her eyes narrowed and she stalked into the barn. "Going along with you was the dumbest thing I've ever done. I should just march out and tell her the truth."

"Please, honey, you don't want to ruin my vacation."

"Don't you honey me. It would serve you right if I turned into another Gloria—trying to force you into getting married. Think how troublesome I could be. You're trapped on the ranch. I could chase you all over the place."

Logan grinned. "Naw, you couldn't be another Gloria. And besides, being married to you wouldn't be half bad. There are worse things in life."

Merrie ground her teeth together. No doubt "worse things" included the plague, pestilence and having the Seattle Mariner's top batter break his arm in the first game of the season. Logan didn't fool her for an instant, he just wanted her to go along with their fake engagement to keep Gloria from bothering him.

"I'd make a lousy wife. You forget I can't cook," she said with artificial sweetness.

"Yeah, that really tears it. You'd have to stay out of the kitchen and promise never to touch the vacuum cleaner. How did you make it explode, anyway?"

"I didn't do anything. That thing is an overpriced piece of junk."

"It is now." Logan refrained from mentioning her sister had successfully operated that "piece of junk" for over four years without exploding it once. He didn't think Merrie would appreciate the reminder.

"I don't want to discuss it," she muttered. "Grandfather wants us to move the cows in the northeast corner—for *real* this time. In other words, no more cozy picnics." She rubbed Sun Spot's nose, whispering to him.

"Merrie-girl...what's this about you getting engaged?" Paul Harding thundered from the door of the barn. "My own granddaughter, and I have to hear it from one of the hands."

Merrie groaned. "Granddad...I know this is a shock, but I can explain."

"Nothing to explain, child. I couldn't be happier." Mr. Harding sounded honestly pleased, and he slapped Logan's back as he strode past. "You're making plans for yourself, outside of this ranch. That's wonderful."

Her face paled, and Logan felt her anguish so clearly, it was as if he had been hurting himself. This wasn't a game to Merrie, it was her life's dream. "Sir, you don't understand. Merrie still wants the ranch," he said urgently.

"Of course she does, son."

Merrie's gaze met his in shared bewilderment.

"Uh, sir?"

Harding turned to his granddaughter with a brief, apologetic shrug. "I've been a stubborn old man, but we'll discuss your ideas for the Bar Nothing as soon as we can. For now, though, you'd better get out on the trail. You've got work to do."

She tucked a strand of hair behind her ear. "I need to talk to grandmother before we leave. I don't want her to think the wrong thing."

"That's all right. I'll explain. We've waited long enough for great grandkids...she'll be real pleased." He left then, with a last approving smile.

Whistling under his breath, Logan watched Merrie, unsure of what to expect—she was unpredictable, to say the least. She might be furious at this turn of events, or wildly delighted. Naturally he was hoping for wildly delighted.

"Honey?"

"Would you stop calling me that?" She lifted a saddle over Sun Spot's back and began fastening the cinch straps. Logan glanced to where Dust Devil stood, ready to go. The bridle Merrie had dropped still lay on the ground, so he walked outside to collect it.

"Thanks," she mumbled, taking the bit and easing it into Sun Spot's mouth.

"Merrie...this is good for you, isn't it?"

"It's a lie."

"Yeah, only you heard what Mr. Harding said...he's going to listen to your plans. That's what you've wanted all along."

"I know." She sighed and rested her forehead against the palomino's white-gold mane. "God, Logan. I've never lied to my family. I wanted to tell him the truth…but I couldn't. This is the first time he's shown any genuine interest in me taking over the ranch.''

Logan rubbed the back of his neck. ''And if you tell him the truth—that we're not engaged—he might back off again…?''

''You heard him. What do you think?''

Her concern was justified—old ideas died hard. Basic, honest values thrived in this part of Montana…along with some old-fashioned ideas about women. It put Logan in a tough spot, because deep down he clung to some of those ideas. For example…a man should protect someone who wasn't as strong. Like Merrie, who was half his size and strength.

Logan told himself that Merrie had an essential strength, unmarked by physical boundaries, but he still didn't want her doing something her body wasn't built to handle. And he didn't want her to do anything dangerous—like breaking a horse.

Damn, he groaned to himself. He'd practically swallowed his tonsils when he learned that was one of her goals—to break the horses on the Bar Nothing. At the same time he admitted her soft voice could tame probably a pride of lions, let alone some horse she'd raised.

''Listen, Merrie. I know you don't want to hide anything from your grandparents, and I admire that. But give it a few days. Maybe it'll open up his mind about you and the ranch.''

''And maybe it won't.''

''Then you're no worse off than before. Besides, honey, it could be fun.''

''You already said that—when you were trying to talk me into an affair.'' Merrie led Sun Spot out of the barn and secured the saddlebags she'd brought down earlier. She tossed him a length of rope, keeping a similar coil for her own use. "Fake engagement or not, I'm not going to bed with you, Logan Kincaid."

"We'll see."

Her chin lifted, as he'd known it would if he made such a flagrant male retort. Merrie's stubbornness came in handy, particularly when she needed a little spunk to fall back on.

"Dream on, city slicker." She swung into Sun Spot's saddle in one, graceful motion. "You won't be so interested after spending the day in a saddle. That tends to kill the romance."

"It doesn't seem to stop ol' Chip."

Merrie's mouth dropped open and she blinked.

"Huh," she muttered.

Logan climbed onto his own horse and gathered the reins. "Yeah...that's what I thought you'd say."

Seven hours later, Logan swung the inevitable rope alongside Dust Devil's neck, listening to the deep-throated bawls of the cattle as they plodded over the hill.

Merrie had enthused about the joys of a well-trained cutting horse, but he hadn't understood until he'd worked a group of cows for the first time. A horse was a horse, right?

Not by a long shot.

Dust Devil didn't really need a rider—Logan would have sworn he could move a herd by himself. And whatever Dust Devil and Sun Spot couldn't take care of, Bandit would handle. Bandit was a terrific cow dog, though he often looked a little goofy with his tongue hanging from the side of his mouth.

Logan took a deep breath, his body relaxed as he moved with the big horse. After just a week he'd begun to automatically check for the Bar Nothing brand on the rumps of each cow. The same for checking fence lines for breaks.

They carried a gadget to staple tags into the cattle's ears and stopped when necessary to accomplish this task. It reassured him to see how cautious Merrie was...after all, she explained, it wasn't smart to take chances around an eleven hundred pound animal with the intellectual capacity of a fence post.

Merrie was right about being connected to the land...it *was* wonderful. And it brought a soul-deep satisfaction. Making rich people richer didn't stack up well against it.

"Say, how big *is* the Bar Nothing?" Logan asked when he'd rejoined Merrie. She'd gone after a couple of cattle in a draw, who now wandered along with the fifty head they'd already collected. They'd push them another half mile into new grazing, and then swing back to the ranch center.

"About six thousand acres."

His hands drew back on the reins and Dust Devil obligingly stopped, though there wasn't any reason for the halt. *Six* thousand *acres?* If Logan had been thinking clearly he would have realized the ranch had to be that big. But still...

Merrie reined in Sun Spot and looked back over her shoulder. "What's wrong?"

"Six thousand?"

"Give or take an acre. We have the exact figures in the ranch records."

"Merrie, nobody could buy that much land on a teacher's salary! It's not possible," Logan said furiously. No wonder her grandfather couldn't get serious about her proposal.

Her mouth twisted with irritation, and he felt a rush of

regret—it wasn't his concern, he shouldn't have said anything to disturb the peace between them.

"I'm not buying the ranch on a teacher's salary," Merrie informed him. "I'm just earning the down payment. Besides, it isn't just my teaching income. I tutor on the side and work here in the summer. My living expenses are almost zero. And my money is invested—not in high stakes stocks or anything, but I'm getting a good return."

· "Honey, I'm sorry..." Logan said, more gently. He wasn't helping either of them by making her angry. "But a few thousand dollars isn't going to—"

"It's more than that." Succinctly she reeled off a figure that made him blink. Merrie had saved considerably more than a "few" thousand dollars, and his perception took another whirling spin.

His normal logic—which tended to operate a beat behind where Merrie was concerned—clicked into gear. On the surface, it seemed unworkable for her to buy the ranch. But anyone determined enough to save that kind of money deserved to be taken seriously.

"Okay," he murmured. "That's impressive. I still don't get the problem—your grandfather could work out a deal where the land reverts to him if things don't work out. He wouldn't lose anything. He could still sell to an outsider."

"Yeah...whatever." She pulled her cowboy hat farther over her eyes, concealing her expression from him.

Logan's chest tightened with anger. He wanted to understand Merrie, not let her hide from him. Deliberately he leaned over and flicked the hat from her head.

"Logan!"

"Talk to me. There's a piece of this puzzle I don't get. Does he want the money that bad? All in one chunk? Is that why he won't sell you the ranch?"

"Of course not." Merrie hesitated, biting her lip so hard he could see a small bead of blood along the edge of her teeth. "It's just…the Bar Nothing is important out here."

"How important?"

Her gaze flicked to him, and then back to her hands. "Logan, ranching isn't the most profitable business, no matter what people think. A lot of folks end up losing everything they've worked a lifetime building."

"Like Harvey?"

"Yeah…like Harvey. Our dude vacations provide an income for a lot of families—a supplement to what they make on their own spreads. And we're building all the time, getting more and more popular."

Logan waited while Merrie stared ahead. Yet he didn't think she was seeing the cattle and the land and sky, but something quite different.

"Folks around here can't afford for the Bar Nothing to have even one bad year," she said starkly. "For any reason. That's what Granddad is afraid of…failing those neighbors who depend on him."

"So it's more than chauvinism."

Sighing, she tugged her hat back on her head. "Yes and no. I think he'd trust one of my brothers with the ranch, but taking a chance on a woman…? No. With so much riding on it, that's too big a risk for him."

"Merrie…I'm sorry."

She shook her head and shivered, though the day was clear and hot. "Under the circumstances, he thinks an outside buyer would have a better chance of keeping things operating smoothly. Someone with big money behind them, to support the ranch through the lean times."

Taking his bandanna from his pocket, Logan wiped the sweat from his face and neck. The dude vacations might seem like fun and games, but they were a vital part of the local economy. And as much as he hated saying it, he had to be honest. "Honey, your grandfather's got a point."

"Does he?" Merrie turned her head, looking thoughtful rather than angry. "I love this ranch…every rock and stick and animal. And I would do anything for the people who depend on us, because they're part of me. Would it be safer in the hands of a stranger, even a stranger with lots of money?"

She was right. In her own way, Merrie was just as right as her stubborn grandfather.

"Well?" she prodded.

"I don't know."

Bandit sat on the ground in front of them, his head cocked with puzzlement as he watched the two humans. Finally he gave a small "woof," encouraging them to get back to work.

Merrie urged Sun Spot forward again and Logan followed, his forehead creased in thought. It was disturbing to realize how important Merrie's dreams were becoming to him.

Maybe even more important than his own.

Chapter Seven

"Surprise!"

"Happy birthday!"

Merrie blushed as confetti was thrown over both her and Logan. The barn they used for dances had been decorated with streamers and wildflowers, and everyone was dressed in their dude ranch best.

"Happy birthday, darling," declared her grandmother, giving her a kiss. "And the best to you, Logan. This is a double celebration because of your engagement."

"That's very nice. Thank you, Mrs. Harding."

"Go on, there. I keep telling you to call me Eva—or Grandma would be fine. You're part of the family now."

"That's...kind of you."

Merrie nudged Logan, annoyed with his stiff formality. For a man who'd enthusiastically thrown himself into an "engagement," he was acting awfully uncomfortable around his prospective in-laws—almost like a real fiancé. Maybe the deception was getting to him. She could only hope.

As for her grandmother…that was a little sticky. The announcement of an engagement must have been quite a surprise following their conversation the previous morning—she distinctly remembered saying she didn't want Logan to fall in love with her, and that he just wanted sex, anyway. Yet Eva Harding hadn't said a word about the abrupt change of face; she'd just smiled serenely and asked if Merrie was happy.

"Happy birthday, darlin'," said a voice, and Merrie spun around.

"Grant! I missed you at the dance on Saturday."

"Sorry about the dance, but I had a sick horse. What's this I heard about you getting married?"

"Oh, yes." Merrie darted a glance at Logan. "Grant Steele, meet Logan Kincaid."

"A pleasure."

"Likewise." Since Logan's face held an expression she'd come to recognize—similar to a bull snorting and pawing the grass—Merrie made a polite excuse to Grant and dragged her "fiancé" to the other side of the barn.

She'd forgotten her birthday. At least…she'd *tried* to forget it. She should have realized her friends and family wouldn't let the big *three-o* slip by that easily.

Blast. It was harder turning thirty years old than pretending she was happily engaged. Actually the "engagement" had been rather enjoyable as long as she didn't think about it as lying. The night before she'd even been able to discuss buying the Bar Nothing with her grandfather, though naturally he'd wanted Logan's input on the proposal.

"This wasn't my idea. Honest," Logan whispered into her ear after a series of well-wishers and cake cutting, and opening the funny little gifts people gave when they didn't really know you, but wanted to be nice.

"You love it," she whispered back. "I mean, take a look at Gloria. You won't have to worry about her bothering you in Seattle...she's about to self-destruct."

"I told you Chip would handle things," Logan said, chuckling.

Gloria and Chip had argued, insulted and taunted their way through the past two days. Neither pulled any punches and they played dirty. But they were in Chip's territory, and he had the home court advantage.

Just then a hand tugged at Merrie's jeans, demanding attention. "Happy birfday."

Merrie bent over and swept the little girl into her arms. "Thanks, Kimmie. I'm glad to see you. Have you and your brother been good this year?"

"Uh-huh. Daddy gave me a pony."

"Oooh...that's exciting." She kissed Kimmie's cheek, inhaling the scent of powder and baby shampoo and feeling a poignant ache around her heart. She wouldn't be having any babies, not for a while at any rate.

"I'm a real cowgirl now," said the child.

"You sure are." Merrie turned. "Logan, meet Grant's daughter, Kimberly."

"Daughter?" Logan brightened considerably. "Oh, he's married. That's nice."

Merrie kissed the child again and scooted her toward the refreshment table. "Actually Grant is a widower," she explained when they were alone again. "His wife died when Kimmie was born."

Her "fiancé" had the grace to look embarrassed. "Sorry to hear that. You must be good friends."

"We practically grew up together. Grant has a ranch just south of the Bar Nothing." Merrie took a bite of birthday cake. Informal parties were fairly common at the ranch—vacationers loved any excuse to celebrate and the Hardings were happy to oblige.

"I haven't seen him around. Does he work as a wrangler?"

"No, but he usually brings the kids to the Saturday barn dance. They get to play with children their own age and he can relax. It's been hard on Grant, raising two kids on his own."

"It's nice he could come to celebrate your birthday."

"And our engagement, don't forget." Merrie grinned mischievously.

Did she mind that Grant Steele believed she was engaged? Logan couldn't tell. The only emotion he'd recognized was the longing in her eyes when she held Kimmie in her arms. Merrie wanted a baby, and turning thirty was a worry to her, because of the biological clock stuff.

"Darlings," Eva Harding said, coming up with a conspiratorial smile. "Why don't you slip away for a private celebration? I have something to help." She held out a basket containing a bottle of champagne and two tall, fluted glasses. "Find a quiet spot outside and toast the moon."

"What a wonderful idea," Logan declared, taking the basket and peering inside with appreciation. Nice…the Hardings knew something about wine. "You're a woman after my own heart."

"Save your charm for my granddaughter. Now scoot before somebody stops you." Mrs. Harding looked significantly in Gloria Scott's direction before walking away, making him laugh.

Everyone—from the Hardings to the guests—were trying to give them privacy. It had evolved into a sporting event. Gloria ambushed either him or Merrie, and suddenly someone appeared, cutting her off like an unruly steer. Even Bandit had gotten into the act, jumping on Gloria's white designer pants with the muddiest feet imaginable.

Poor Bandit.

Her shrieking had bewildered him worse than any stampede. Then she'd jumped backward and landed in the horse trough. Ever helpful, Bandit had been there to lick her cheek when she came up for air, only to get shrieked at again.

And Chip...he'd remained sitting on the fence rail, chewing on a piece of straw and watching the whole thing.

"Why didn't you do something?" Gloria had screeched at him, crawling from the trough with her blond hair draggled in spikes down her face and her white silk outfit turned an interesting shade of algae green. "Just look at me!"

Chip had methodically cut another plug of tobacco to chew. "That's why folks love it here...lots of activity," he'd murmured reflectively before stuffing it inside his lip. "Always something to do."

"I'm paying you to take care of me."

"Naw...the Hardings are payin' me, ma'am. You're just an oversize pain in the butt."

Just thinking about it made Logan want to howl. Gloria had actually been incoherent. Not speechless, *incoherent.* Then sweet, generous Merrie had tried to comfort her.

"Logan? What's so funny?"

Merrie nudged him and he turned his head, grinning. "I was thinking about this morning...when Gloria tried to push you into the horse trough."

"Oh, God." Merrie's cheeks turned a faint shade of apricot pink. "Honest, she tripped into that cow pie. I didn't have anything to do with it aside from getting out of the way.''

"That's what made it so good."

"Aren't you worried?" Merrie looked a little worried herself, and a cute frown creased the space over her eyes. "You said that Gloria is the boss's daughter. They could make all kinds of trouble for you."

"Naw." Logan put his arm around her shoulder and pushed her toward the door. "They need me a lot more than I need them." It was true, he acknowledged to himself, a little puzzled by the realization. No matter what happened, the company needed him to return to work, a lot more than he needed to go back.

"But—"

"Honey, I really don't want to talk about the office. Where can we go for the privacy Grandma mentioned?"

"I see she's Grandma only when it's convenient," Merrie grumbled, allowing herself to be drawn farther from the light and activity of the barn. "You're an opportunist, Logan Kincaid. You have no scruples."

"Me? Nonsense." Logan laced their fingers together. "You don't object to missing part of your party, do you? If that's the problem, we can go right back in—maybe we can find some more candles and sing 'Happy Birthday' again."

She looked at him blackly. In the moonlight his grin was just as sexy as it was in full daylight. "You're on thin ice, Kincaid. I might just push you into the bull paddock and leave you there."

His chuckle was low and seductive. "I happen to know that mellow old bull is just for show. The Bar Nothing uses semen from a prize-winning bull they've only seen in a video—according to the boss's *grand*daughter, that is."

"A little knowledge is a dangerous thing."

"Come on, honey, let's crack that bottle from your grandmother. I've never seen such a clear sky. It deserves a toast." Logan kissed her temple and she shivered—he didn't fool her for a second about any toast.

"O...kay," she said reluctantly. Actually her mind was the only reluctant part of her—her body was screaming, *What are you waiting for?*

She had to be careful...her body was screaming for a lot of reasons. Hunger for a baby. A general frustration at being told to wait for years and years while she satisfied a different need. It wasn't just Logan...yet when his leg brushed hers and a charge of electric awareness shot to her stomach, it was hard to remember anything else.

"I'll get a quilt from the house," she murmured. "Wait here."

"You'll come back, right? You won't chicken out?"

"Nothing is going to happen, but I'm *not* a coward."

"Sure." He stayed right on her heels as she walked into the ranch house, obviously doubtful. Merrie scowled, she wasn't a coward and *nothing* was going to happen. A pair of counterfeit fiancés could toast the moon without getting carried away.

But just to be sure, she handed him the quilt and took a deep breath. "I thought we'd pick a place out by the tents. It's nice up there."

Logan tucked the quilt under his arm. He shook his head and smiled. "No, let's try the hill behind the house. It's much more private."

Merrie scowled again. Getting private with Logan wasn't a good idea. In fact, it was a damned lousy idea. "Believe me, we *don't* need privacy."

"Sure we do."

"No. Please, Logan, don't push. Not tonight." She was too vulnerable, with conflicting needs and questions that couldn't be answered.

"Honey?" Logan tipped her chin up, his face no longer laughing, but soberly intent. "It's okay. It's your birthday, and I'll play the way you want. No kissing."

"None at all?" She eyed him suspiciously.

"Yes."

Merrie believed him, but she wasn't sure if it was any better than the alternative. At least when Logan kissed her, she didn't think. Heck, she hardly breathed. There wasn't room for uncomfortable thoughts and useless speculation.

He held out his hand. "Coming?"

Maybe the champagne would numb her brain. "Uh, sure."

"I like this," Logan said contentedly. They'd been lying there for hours, counting stars while the rest of the ranch slept.

"You do?"

"Yeah." He took a sip of now-flat champagne then looked back at the sky. "Not as much as kissing you, but it's not bad. Relaxing."

"Hmm." Merrie lay in the opposite direction from him, her feet near his head. "I like it, too."

"Oh, good. I'm glad."

Bandit was the happiest of them both. He had a comfortable spot between the two humans, and Merrie's loving touch. Every now and then the shepherd gave a snuffling sigh of satisfaction and inched closer to her...an action Logan fully understood. He wouldn't mind her rubbing his ears, and then moving on to other portions of his body that needed attention.

"Tell me something," Merrie said, sitting up and pouring herself another glass of champagne. "Why are you so dead set against marriage? Your family might have had some bad luck in that direction, but that doesn't mean you couldn't make it work."

"Why, are you interested?"

Merrie choked, spraying champagne across his legs. "Good God, no. It was just a theoretical question…like do you think intelligent life exists on other planets?"

Her vehement denial stung his pride. "Thanks. I'm not the worst husband you could have."

"Right, you don't smoke, gamble or rob convenience stores for a living. That's quite a recommendation."

"Sheesh." Logan sat up and glared. "If I ever do get married it won't be to someone like—" He stopped, because even in the moonlight he could see her eyes flashing, and he had the feeling he was about to make a mistake.

"Like me?" Merrie said, her words clipped.

"Well, I'd want someone calmer. Not that I'm saying you aren't stable, but I've seen relationships with someone who's a bit hot-tempered. Life is always a drama."

"Oh, you want a boring wife. You should have said so. When you get home, add 'boring' to your list."

The wife list.

Logan had hoped she'd forgotten that stupid piece of paper.

Damn. If he hadn't said the wrong thing, they could still be peacefully sipping wine and counting the stars. But he'd screwed things up, and kept making it worse.

"Honey, please, I think you're very special. Maybe if things were different…" He shrugged.

"Different? Not a chance," she snapped. "Heaven

knows, I don't even have one of the qualities you require in a wife.''

''Why are you so hung up on that list?''

Merrie closed her mouth tightly.

''I agree it was dumb. But Sully and I were drunk—he'd just signed his divorce papers and was bitter as hell. He didn't want me to repeat his mistakes.''

''Fine. Make your own mistakes.'' Merrie jumped to her feet, too restless to think straight. ''I'm going to bed,'' she muttered. ''Come, Bandit.''

She slapped her hand on her leg to encourage him, but the shepherd merely cocked his head in confusion and yipped.

''Fine, stay if you want. Men always stick together.''

''Merrie...wait.''

At his urgent plea she paused, putting a hand to her stomach. It wasn't Logan's fault. She'd overreacted. She had too much to deal with—too much to lose by making the wrong decisions. And her thirtieth birthday was the last night to sit under a moonlit sky and think about her dreams.

''I'm sorry, honey.'' Lightly Logan put his hands on her arms and rubbed. Her wineglass slipped from her fingers to the grass below and she swayed against him, lured by the heat of his body. ''My pride got hurt,'' he whispered. ''So I hurt you back. The truth is, I think you're wonderful.''

''Logan...'' she sighed, and his arms slid around her waist, pulling her to him. She felt him, the hardness of his thighs against her bottom, and the growing bulge of his arousal. ''Is...is that what we were arguing about?''

''This?''

His hips moved and she moaned. ''Yes.''

''I've never wanted a woman as much as I want you,''

he whispered into her neck. "And you want me. It's the one part of our engagement we're not faking."

Ice condensed in Merrie's stomach. That was the problem—a part of her wished they weren't faking anything. It scared her. Falling in love with Logan would be so foolish. He was smart and ambitious and had New York City written into his future.

New York.

Miles and miles of concrete. No meadows or endless, unbroken skies. People said the snow in New York wasn't even white, it was gray. The Big Apple might be a wonderful city, but she was sure she'd suffocate there.

It shouldn't worry her; she was the last woman Logan would ever marry. But if the impossible happened—if they fell in love with each other—then she'd have to choose between him and the ranch. Merrie shivered for a far different reason than sensual awareness.

"Don't worry, honey." His hands still soothed her...warmed her. "I promised."

Promised?

Oh, his promise not to kiss her.

"Lie down again," he breathed, easing them back to the quilt, but this time holding her tightly to him. It was sexual and comforting and so achingly tender that her throat hurt with suppressed emotion.

Merrie put her arm across Logan and closed her eyes, breathing the cool night air...breathing his scent. He flipped a corner of the quilt over her legs and she heard the tinkle of his wineglass as it went flying.

"Uh, those weren't family heirlooms, were they?" he asked.

"Nope."

"Good." He stroked his fingers over her hair, playing with the long strands. "I think your grandmother would forgive me, but I wouldn't want to be responsible for breaking something special.''

Family...Merrie pressed her palm over Logan's heart. It beat with a steady, strong rhythm. ''Tell me something,'' she whispered. ''Why didn't you come to Christmas dinner when Lianne invited you?''

She could tell the question surprised him. His body tensed, and for an instant Merrie thought she'd ruined everything again. He'd get angry and offended and they'd fight. Risking a peek, she looked at his face, staring at a lone cloud drifting across the moon.

A ragged sigh welled from his chest. ''I hate to admit it, but I was...embarrassed.''

''Embarrassed? Because your housekeeper was inviting you to dinner?'' She took a deep breath, counting to ten and waiting for an answer. There *had* to be an answer—for all his status house, and status job, and status life, she knew Logan wasn't a snob.

''Jeez, Merrie,'' he muttered. ''That wasn't the reason. I don't know how to act around a friendly, normal family. I would have made everyone uncomfortable and spoiled your Christmas.''

Merrie blinked. It was the last thing she'd expected to hear. ''But you have a family, don't you? At least a brother—Sully, right?''

''Yeah, I have a brother and a couple of sisters, and my parents are still very much alive. Unfortunately they never got divorced. They're still destroying what's left of their lives by staying together.''

The weary, bitter acceptance in his voice made tears burn in her eyes.

''I don't expect you to understand,'' he said. ''Your family isn't like anything I've seen. God, you actually *like* each other.'' He cupped her cheek in the palm of his hand and stroked his thumb across her lips.

''Logan?'' she whispered.

''You want to know why it's so important I make a success of myself? Simple—I was the dirt poor kid from the wrong side of town, Merrie. My dad wasn't unemployed, he just didn't want to work. And the police…they had a regular stop at my house every Friday and Saturday night to break up drunken fights between my parents. The neighbors were always complaining about them disturbing the peace.''

The pain in his words cut through Merrie's heart and she kissed Logan's throat. None of it mattered to her— not the poverty or unhappy family.

''It's all right,'' she whispered.

''No, it isn't. Hell, I didn't want you to know all that stuff. I should have kept my mouth shut, but I'm having trouble doing that tonight.''

''Logan, you should be proud of yourself,'' she insisted quietly. ''You got through college and you work hard. I may not agree with using money as a scorecard, but you've changed your life—not too many people do that.''

He didn't say anything for a long while, but the tension in his body eased. ''You're amazing, do you know that Merrie Foster?''

''I'm just me.''

''That's what I mean.''

Chapter Eight

"Honey, wake up."

Merrie mumbled something and curled tighter against him. It was pleasant, but it didn't help matters.

"We fell asleep. It's morning." Logan consulted his watch. "Damn, they'll think we eloped. It's almost eight-thirty."

"Can't be." Her eyes stayed closed. "I never oversleep."

"There's always a first time."

Grumbling, Merrie rolled over and sat up. "It's morning," she said with some surprise.

"Yeah, that's what I've been saying. I'll bet they've sent out the posse or lynching party, or whatever it is they do to misbehaving suitors."

"You didn't misbehave—you were a perfect gentleman." Was it Logan's imagination, or did she sound a little disappointed about the "gentleman" part?

"Well, I *thought* about misbehaving."

"Huh…" She yawned and stretched, her body arched

gracefully. "If thinking was against the law, they'd have to lock up the entire male population. You're safe."

But for how long?

Logan squirmed, because seeing Merrie stretch was guaranteed to make him even hotter and more uncomfortable, and he'd already been pretty hot and uncomfortable. Her hair was all rumpled from sleeping in his arms. She wasn't wearing a scrap of makeup, though with her flawless complexion, she really didn't need any. Her green shirt was practical, yet it matched her eyes. Her jeans were quite a turn-on, but it was the woman who made the jeans, rather than the other way around.

He cleared his throat. "We'd better find the Hardings and explain nothing happened to us. I like your grandparents. I don't want them to worry."

"Okay."

She put out her hand and he tugged her to her feet. Fractured light glinted off the pieces of the wineglass they'd broken, and they collected them with the basket and the quilt they'd been sleeping on. But before Merrie could leave, he caught her shoulders.

"Honey, about the things I said last night…I didn't mean to hurt you."

Her eyes regarded him soberly. Silently.

"You really are special."

Merrie sighed and bit the tip of her tongue to keep from saying something she'd regret. Special? Maybe, but not special enough. And she was a fool for worrying about it. The ranch was solid, real, not a fleeting moment of passion that would break her heart in the end.

She shrugged. "It's okay. I didn't mean to hurt your pride, either."

"I just want you so much, I don't think straight," he

murmured, stroking his thumbs across her cheeks and lips.

"Please, Logan. Don't talk about that."

"Why, honey? We aren't a couple of teenagers with runaway hormones, we're adults. We can talk about our needs."

"Right, we're *adults* with runaway hormones. Talk about it? That's like putting a lighted match to gasoline." Merrie stepped back, shaking her head determinedly. "Let's go tell everyone we didn't elope—though I doubt anybody's worried about it. They must have seen us from the house."

"If I was your grandfather, I'd have worried more about seeing us wrapped up together before the wedding."

"You know something, Logan?" she said, glancing at him as they walked down the hill. "You're a fraud. A prude in disguise."

"I am not."

"Sure you are." Merrie surveyed him up and down. His hair was mussed, beard shadow darkened his skin, and his eyes were sleepily compelling. *All* man. Sex incarnated. And she decided he was still disgustingly perfect—prude or not.

"I am definitely *not* a prude. That's a terrible thing to call a man."

"Huh. It's all fine and modern to have an affair with me, but if it was your daughter being seduced, you'd flip out and call the marines."

"I'm never going to have a daughter."

Her lips tightened. "Good for you."

"Hey, it's not a crime," Logan protested. "I'm rotten with children. The kids in the neighborhood call me an ogre, did you know that? Would you wish that on some poor, unsuspecting child? The Ogre of Nisqually Drive for a father. What a nightmare.''

She was about to declare he deserved the title when the kitchen door opened and her grandmother appeared, full of smiles and twinkles. ''Come in and have some breakfast. I wondered if you'd ever wake up.''

''Sorry, Mrs. Harding.'' Logan glanced at Merrie and saw her mouth twist wryly. ''Grandma,'' he amended. ''We didn't intend to fall asleep out there—blame it on the champagne.''

Eva laughed and investigated the basket she'd given them the night before. She pulled out the bottle, which still held a fair amount of wine. ''I think you got drunk on each other. Oh, my…I remember when Paul and I were first married.'' A tender smile curved her mouth. ''We'd sit out on that same hill and talk and talk.''

''We talked all right,'' Merrie muttered.

''Eat, you two,'' Eva urged, not seeming to notice Merrie's discomfort.

The table was laden with crisp waffles and ham and country fried potatoes, accompanied by such treats as strawberries and peach preserves and home-churned butter. A feast by any standards, but the combination of hard work and fresh Montana air had put a healthy edge to his appetite.

A pleased smile grew on his face, despite his concerns about Merrie and the subterfuge they were perpetuating. He'd never enjoyed himself so much.

The Bar Nothing might entertain ''dudes'' to earn extra money, but cattle were their business. They didn't play around, they fiercely protected their animals and conducted a full range of ranching activities. It was a far cry from making rich people richer, and lots more satisfying than manipulating stock portfolios, where money existed on paper as a kind of game. More and more, he understood Merrie's passion for owning the Bar Nothing.

"Where did you and Mr. Harding meet?" Logan asked, gently pushing Merrie into a chair.

Eva joined them for a cup of coffee, a faraway expression on her lined face. "Paul had just graduated from an agricultural college in California, and I was traveling by train to visit a cousin in Sacramento. I got off at the wrong station and asked this giant of a man for help. He took one look at me and said 'You're the girl I'm going to marry.'"

"I said no such thing," Paul Harding denied as he walked into the kitchen.

"Don't listen to him, Logan," Eva ordered. "He doesn't want you to know what a hopeless romantic he used to be."

"I was never romantic, and I remember exactly what I told you." The elder man smiled. "I said you'd need a better sense of direction if you expected to marry me and live in Montana."

"You were always cocky," she scolded, but there was no anger in her words, only love.

Logan grinned and looked at Merrie. Though she must have heard it a hundred times, she was leaning forward, her eyes soft as she listened to the teasing story.

"How long before you actually got married?" he asked.

Paul shook his head sorrowfully. "Five whole days. It always takes Eva a while to make up her mind."

Mrs. Harding shook her head. "Listen to him talk. You'd think it was all my idea to wait."

Five days? Logan was stunned. It was obvious the Hardings had enjoyed a long, happy life, but how could you get to know another person so quickly? Enough to be sure you wanted to spend a lifetime together? Five days…most people took longer deciding what kind of car to buy.

Even if he believed in marriage, he'd take a lot longer to decide. Wouldn't he?

God, he was confused.

A week ago he would have said there wasn't a chance in hell he'd ever think of getting married. Now he wasn't so sure; meeting Merrie had changed everything. He could almost believe in a happy marriage with her. And it wasn't only because she was beautiful…it was because of everything that made her so special—her laughter and determination and honesty, the way she had of making everything fun.

Marriage might not be that bad.

Right?

Of course, he might be a little euphoric. Vacations could do that to a person. Yet he could almost see it working.

Aware of Merrie's gaze upon him, Logan took a long swallow of coffee. He couldn't quite put his finger on it, but she seemed different this morning. Uneasy. He didn't blame her—they both disliked the deception they were playing on her grandparents. It had started out innocently and snowballed into a gigantic muddle.

"Er, what are we assigned to do today, sir?" he asked Mr. Harding. "I know we're late getting started."

"Late indeed," scolded Paul, though his eyes gleamed. "But that's all right. You can ride the fence lines to the west."

Merrie straightened in her chair and hastily swallowed the bite of waffle in her mouth. She didn't mind occasional busywork when they were keeping vacationers happy, but she didn't enjoy doing it for no reason.

"Granddad—the dudes just moved the cattle in that section two days ago, and you had Spike ride the fences at the same time. They're fine."

"Check 'em again."

"But—"

"Now, Merrie," he chided gently. "Half the day is gone already, and you've both worked hard since getting here. You and Logan just have a relaxing time together. Don't worry about the ranch for once. It'll keep."

"I...okay." She glowered and bit her tongue against another protest. Paul Harding was the boss. She might be a relative, yet like everyone else working on the Bar Nothing, she did what he said.

"Yes," urged her grandmother. "You should enjoy yourselves more. You only get engaged once."

Merrie pressed her fingernails into her palm. She'd gotten herself into this mess—with a little help from Logan—and she'd have to get herself out. Only how? That was the big question. They could pretend to have a fight and break off the engagement, except that would mean telling another lie. On the other hand, revealing the truth didn't seem any easier.

"We'll be happy to ride the fence lines," Logan said, putting his hand over hers and squeezing softly. "Maybe we could have another picnic."

Merrie snatched her hand away. "I don't think so."

"Wonderful," Eva enthused, as though Merrie hadn't said anything. "I'll pack a lunch right now."

Swell.

She gave Logan a look that no one could interpret as friendly. Luckily he was the only one watching. "Uh, finish your breakfast. I'll meet you at the corral in an hour," she told him.

He smiled complacently.

* * *

"Merrie?"

Merrie peered over the edge of the loft. It was peaceful and shadowy this high in the barn. Maybe if she kept quiet, Logan wouldn't be able to find her and she could spend the day without his annoying, upsetting presence.

Except he wasn't that annoying, and she was mostly upset by daydreams of brown-haired, brown-eyed children, all with Logan Kincaid's devastating grin.

"Honey?"

She sighed. "Here."

Logan appeared in the doorway, silhouetted by the brighter daylight outside the barn. "Where?"

"Up here." She leaned farther out, holding on to one of the roof beams. "I had some extra time, so I've been searching for Pidge's family."

He found the steps to the loft and climbed up. "And who is Pidge?"

"Pidge is a cat—the best mouser ever born," Merrie explained. "She had her babies a few days ago, but I haven't been able to find where she's hidden them. Mother cats are extremely protective, and she doesn't like all the comings and goings of visitors. You can't blame her, it's instinctive."

"This seems like a good hiding place. Very...private."

Merrie groaned. She recognized that particular look in Logan's eyes. The close intimacy of the loft was the last place she wanted to be when he was thinking about privacy. "We'd better head out," she said quickly. "Grandfather wants those fence lines checked."

"No rush. They just want us to spend the day together. Our engagement has been awfully nice—everyone gives us time alone. It's so considerate of them."

"Our fake engagement," she felt obliged to point out, rather unnecessarily since Logan wasn't likely to get married to anyone, especially her.

Logan leaned against a bale of hay and glanced around. "It's nice up here. Tidy, practical...I like that about the Bar Nothing. There aren't any neglected corners."

"Thanks." Merrie squirmed restlessly. She'd have to climb over his legs to get to the ladder, something he'd probably realized when he sat there. His "no kissing" promise had been limited to her birthday, and it wasn't her birthday anymore. Which was a problem, because she *wanted* Logan to kiss her.

No doubt about it—she was an idiot.

Though he'd apologized for his comments the night before, it didn't change the truth of what he'd said. *If* Logan ever got married, it would be to someone completely opposite than herself. Someone calm and unemotional, who didn't turn everything into a "drama."

It made a peculiar kind of sense, considering what he'd revealed of his childhood. Drunken fights between his parents. The humiliation a child would feel at having the police come to the door for any reason. Merrie Foster— with her tendency to speak before thinking—was the last woman he'd want for a wife.

Yet all that stuff about being the Ogre of Nisqually Drive...did that mean he was thinking about having a family? Was he questioning his ability to be a good father? Interesting...not that she cared, of course. But it was very interesting.

"I take it you didn't find Pidge?" Logan asked.

"Er, no."

"Do you think she's all right?"

Merrie played with the ends of the bandanna tied

around her neck. "She's been coming up to the house to eat. Pidge just doesn't like to share her kittens till they're older. Cats are very independent, you know. Naturally when females are in heat things get pretty rowdy."

Babbling, she thought. She was babbling because Logan was getting closer and closer to her heart; and she didn't want him anywhere near that vulnerable organ.

Logan smiled lazily. "Isn't it great the way sex stirs things up?"

Warmth burned in her cheeks. "Sex must be better for the male, than the female. After all, it's the female who ends up pregnant—not too many tomcats stick around to play papa."

"Maybe they don't think they'd be any good with babies," Logan suggested, and they both knew he wasn't talking about tomcats.

Merrie regarded the toes of her boots. "I'll bet if they stuck around, they'd discover they weren't that bad with…kittens."

"I don't know. Papas lack the necessary equipment to keep babies happy." Logan sent a significant look to her bustline.

"Excuses, excuses." She took a shaky breath and crawled over his outstretched legs. "I don't want to talk about cats or their sex lives. Let's get going."

"I don't want to talk, period." He deftly caught one of the belt loops of her jeans and tipped her backward to the floor.

"Logan!"

"Merrie!" he mimicked in the same tone. "I just want a private moment with my fiancée." He leaned over her, tracing the curve of her face with his finger.

"We just spent the night together," she said carelessly. "What more could you want?"

"Hmm. I must have slept through the fun part of that activity. Let's try a repeat on that pile of hay in the corner. I'm sure I'll remember this time."

Merrie wanted to be angry. She really did. Men had their minds permanently engraved with one thought...*sex*. Though, she had to admit she'd been guilty of that herself lately. Except...it wasn't just sex. It was so easy talking to Logan, laughing and sharing her dreams. Even fighting with him was fun, though she preferred the alternative.

Why couldn't he see that? Fights didn't have to be destructive. You could disagree with a person and still care about them...still have a normal, happy life.

Damn.

The closer she got to Logan, the more she started thinking impossible things. Where was her common sense? She didn't want to choose between Logan and the ranch, and she'd have to choose if they fell in love.

"How about it, honey?" He fiddled with the top button of her shirt, and for the life of her, she couldn't push him away.

"You don't really expect me to say yes?"

He shrugged. "It was worth a try."

"Well, think again." But an unwilling smile brightened her face, and he kissed the corner of her mouth.

"You don't sound convinced," Logan whispered. "How about it? Everyone should have a roll in the hay to remember in their old age."

"Huh. Rolling in the hay isn't everything it's cracked up to be. It's messy and it pokes you—especially when you aren't wearing any clothes."

"Really?" Logan looked at the golden mass of straw with a speculative eye. "Are you speaking from experience, or did someone tell you about it?"

"That's privileged information."

"Even for a fiancé?"

"You aren't—"

All at once Merrie froze, hearing a sound in the barn below them. They both turned their heads and listened warily.

One of the horses neighed.

A board creaked.

A scrabbling sound came from the staircase, and Bandit's friendly face appeared over the top step.

The shepherd "woofed" and they laughed with relief. It would be hard enough coming clean about their supposed engagement, without the truth being accidentally overheard.

"I think Bandit is anxious for us to get out riding," Merrie whispered. She started to edge away from Logan, only to have him catch her arms.

"Merrie...you seem different today. Is something wrong?"

She raised one eyebrow. "Aside from the fact I'm lying to my grandparents and friends? Or the minor detail that I'm thirty years old and am no closer to owning the ranch other than a discussion with Grandfather? And that—"

"Okay," Logan said quickly. "I get the picture. To be honest, I was afraid you were still angry about last night, but I guess you have bigger worries."

To her surprise, Merrie almost giggled, because one of her "big" worries was pressing alongside the worn denim covering her thigh...and Logan didn't even seem aware of his condition. She looped her arms around his neck and smiled. He was a nice man. A little mixed up and dangerous to her peace of mind, but darned nice all the same.

"I'm not angry about anything."

"Good."

The warmth and closeness of the loft had put a damp sheen on his upper lip, and Merrie fought the temptation to lick it off. It would be erotic and sinfully delicious. And it would start his thoughts headed toward rolling in the hay again.

"We'd better go down," she murmured. "The horses are saddled and waiting."

"Yeah, I guess we'd better," Logan agreed, but he didn't move any more than she did.

"We're not accomplishing anything."

"I wouldn't say that." And he rubbed against her thigh in a way that said he'd never forgotten the dominantly male part of his anatomy, he'd just been biding his time for a better moment to bring it to her attention.

"Logan," she moaned, because her resistance was getting dangerously low and it was dirty pool to flirt with her when they'd slept in each other arms. Her body was still tuned to his, her senses imprinted with his scent and warmth.

"Have I told you how grateful I am?"

"Grateful?" She looked at him suspiciously, certain this was just a new ploy to get inside her jeans.

"Yeah...grateful I found you on that tree house. I could have been bored out of my skull right now, instead of having so much fun."

"Oh." Merrie felt ridiculously pleased. "Even though I nearly burned down the house?"

"Even though." He kissed her mouth...a light, nibbling kiss that made her hungry for more.

"Not that I meant to burn anything."

"I know," Logan soothed. The ache in his groin demanded release, yet he'd never enjoyed a kiss so much. "You were trying to help Lianne."

"She's very, uh, sweet," Merrie murmured. "Lots nicer than me. And she's not dumb, she just has terrible judgment about men. Of course, I don't know that my judgment is any better."

Logan hesitated. No matter what Merrie said, she was acting different this morning. She didn't always meet his eyes and she seemed nervous. It was a subtle change, but definite.

He forced a grin. "Thanks for the vote of confidence. At the moment, I happen to think your judgment is terrific. And by the way…I think you're plenty nice—I like you exactly the way you are."

"Thank you," Merrie said between long kisses, and the velvet strokes of his tongue into her mouth.

He cupped his hands over her breasts, lightly rubbing the crowning centers.

Merrie arched, gasping at the sensation. Each time it was better. She wanted his touch…his mouth on her nipples, suckling and teasing her. Most of all, she wanted the emptiness in her abdomen to go away, the throbbing heat that left her edgy and needy whenever they stopped. Yet she couldn't…it was too risky getting involved in that way.

The sound of horses in the distance was almost a relief, because it meant an end to the exquisite torture.

"Damnation. Company," Logan breathed.

Merrie blinked, and the dazed expression slowly faded from her eyes. "Who could that be?"

They both wiggled to the edge of the loft, looking down in time to see Gloria come barreling into the barn as if a pack of wolves was behind her. Chip followed at a much more leisurely pace, first stopping to tie their mounts to the corral fence.

"I told you to keep your tail put, and that's what I meant," Chip said.

"You boorish clod. I have every intention of keeping my 'tail' exactly where I please."

"On this ranch, you'll stay put if I tell you. We were chasin' a hurt steer. No place for a useless piece of city fluff."

Merrie choked and clapped her hand across her mouth. Gloria looked as though she'd been sprayed in the face by a skunk.

"Why do you keep saying that? I'm not useless," she shrieked. "I'm not."

Chip obviously wasn't impressed. "Do tell?"

Beside her, Logan was shaking with suppressed laughter. He caught a rope looped over the rafter and pulled himself upright.

"No, don't!" Merrie warned, but it was too late.

The rope released a trap door—dropping their section of the loft by a pair of hinges. Fortunately they tumbled into a pile of loose hay, which cushioned their landing.

Gloria shrieked again, but Chip just nodded casually. "Howdy, Red. Wondered where you got to last night. Quite a party."

Merrie didn't move, she just smashed her face into Logan's chest. It was unkind, really. Gloria had "lost" Logan to another women, and then she'd been taunted by a tobacco-chewing cowboy, told she was a pain in the rear end, and dumped in a horse trough. On top of which, she'd been forced to attend the other woman's "engagement" party. Now this…Merrie could almost feel sorry for her.

"Honey, are you okay?" Logan asked.

"Fine," she said, her voice muffled in his shirt. "How about you?"

"Terrific. You're making a habit of landing on me. I enjoy it. Did you lose your top this time?" he asked hopefully.

"Rat." Merrie pinched his side and he yelped.

"Hey, it was an innocent question. And you know me—I'm always willing to sacrifice my clothing for your modesty." He made it sound as if she'd regularly go nude without his helpful contributions.

"Right. You're a regular prince." She hauled herself to a sitting position and tossed her hair over her shoulder. A quick glance at Gloria surprised her—instead of the rage and contempt Merrie had expected, she seemed wistful as she watched them together.

"Hi, everyone," Logan said, climbing to his feet. He shook clinging bits of hay from his clothing and hair, then helped Merrie do the same. "Hate to drop and run, but we've got fences to ride. You understand, I'm sure."

"Yup." Chip's gaze settled on the front of Merrie's blue shirt. "I could tell you were gettin' all-fired up to go somewhere."

Logan turned Merrie around and fastened the five buttons he'd managed to *un*fasten in the loft. He liked Chip, but some things were personal—and Merrie's lacy peach bra was one of them.

"You said one of the animals was hurt?" Merrie asked, her cheeks turning hot.

"Not too bad. Broke through a fence and caught his neck on the barbed wire—ornery as sin, too. Then Miss City Britches decided to go down and powder her nose in the middle of roundin' him up."

"I did nothing of the sort," Gloria snapped resentfully.

"You didn't give me a chance to explain. You...you dumb *cowboy*."

A concerned frown creased Merrie's forehead. "Miss Scott, I'm afraid you don't understand. We have to protect our—"

"Honey," Logan interrupted hastily. "This is something Gloria and Chip should settle between themselves."

"But—"

"No!" He propelled her toward the barn door. "We have work to do. Picnics to enjoy. Our own business to mind." He whispered the last part and Merrie's expression became even more bewildered.

"But this *is* my business," she insisted quietly. "A dude ranch can't take chances with safety."

Logan waited until she'd climbed onto Sun Spot, before mounting Dust Devil. "This has nothing to do with the ranch. Believe me."

"Nothing?" Merrie reluctantly urged Sun Spot to follow him, her face still stubbornly argumentative. "It has everything to do with the ranch. If Gloria did something dangerous, then I can't let it happen again."

"It won't." Logan slapped the reins, urging his horse into an easy canter. He waited until they'd crossed the first hill before pulling Dust Devil back to a slow walk.

She made a disgusted sound. "How do you know it won't? Nothing should have happened in the first place. I know we make everyone sign a waiver of responsibility, but that doesn't mean we're careless. We do everything possible to protect our guests."

"Honey..." he said patiently. "You're great at reading an animal's body language, so tell me what Gloria and Chip *weren't* saying with their mouths?"

Her jaw dropped. "I...that's ridiculous."

"Stranger things have happened. As for protecting

Gloria…if you've taken a look at Chip's hat, you'll see he's been using plenty of protection. At this rate, he'll have to restock his protection before the week is over.''

Merrie rolled her eyes.

''I know, it boggles the imagination.'' Logan shook his head. He was still astonished himself—obviously, Chip wasn't too discriminating when it came to women. ''But it seems pretty clear. Being inexperienced in that direction, you might not recognize the signs.''

''You don't know anything about my experience,'' Merrie scolded. ''And I think you're nuts.'' But her voice held some doubt and her lips twitched.

''It's like Conan the Barbarian meets Snow White's wicked stepmother. Although…come to think of it, they might be a perfect match.''

''Stop it.'' Merrie giggled. ''I'm sure Gloria has her good points.''

''Name one.''

''Uh, well…'' She bit the inside of her mouth, trying to think of a positive quality in the other woman. ''She's very…that is…I like her car.''

''Ah-hah!'' He grinned triumphantly. ''You have a weakness for expensive cars. I knew it. Next thing you know, you'll want a red sports car for an engagement present.''

''Huh. I didn't say I wanted one, just that I liked it,'' Merrie asserted. ''As for Gloria—you know her better than I do. You must have something nice to say about her.''

Logan flashed Merrie a warm grin. ''Yeah…she gave me a great excuse to come to Montana. And I'm really grateful.''

''Oh.''

He could tell she was pleased. Her eyes went down,

she bit her lip to keep from smiling and an apricot flush tinged her cheeks.

"Honey?"

"I'm glad you're having a good time."

"Thanks."

Logan urged Dust Devil closer, then reached out and stroked the fiery softness of Merrie's braid as it fell across her shoulder. Beneath his fingers he felt the firm curves cupped by her lacy bra. He drew a sharp breath, reminded of the activity Gloria and Chip had ended.

"Of course," he said slowly. "I'd enjoy myself even more if we could just—"

"Shut up, Logan," said Merrie sweetly. She spurred Sun Spot ahead, breaking their brief contact. "You should learn to quit while you're ahead."

Chapter Nine

Later that night, Logan leaned against the wall and chewed on a piece of hay. It was the last barn dance before folks left on Sunday, and everyone was having a terrific time.

Everyone except him, that is.

Merrie was out on the floor, dancing the polka with Grant Steele and laughing like she didn't have a care in the world. Hell, she wasn't *Steele's* fiancée.

She isn't your *fiancée, either,* nagged his conscience. *Not for real.*

She wasn't actually neglecting him, but she'd spread her attention pretty thin for most of the evening. Talking, teasing, *flirting*. Nobody was left sitting in a corner—she mixed couples, encouraged shy guests to participate and served as a dance partner whenever necessary.

There wasn't an unmarried man in the place who could keep his eyes off her, and a few of the married ones were watching as well.

She flitted around, encouraged him to join in the square

dancing, then flitted off again. Yet Logan couldn't help noticing she spent a lot of time with Grant Steele and his children, and it didn't take a genius to realize the widowed rancher would be a perfect husband for Merrie.

Grant was a family man. He loved kids and he'd happily give Merrie a dozen more if that's what she wanted. He'd grown up on a ranch, knew the business inside and out and was a horse breeder to boot. Her grandparents approved of him, too. And he lived next door...so to speak. Perfect.

Damn.

Logan hated the jealousy nagging at him. It just seemed so ominously familiar. His mother had done the same thing...played games to make his father jealous. Flirting with any male she could find. Taunting him with his failures as a husband and man.

Stop, he ordered, slugging a glass of cold lemonade down his throat. Merrie wouldn't do that...would she? He watched her whirl around the wood floor and wondered. It was an arrogant question, yet it spun around in his head, searching for an answer.

"Oh, my," she gasped as they finished their dance a few feet away. "I love the polka." She was breathless from the energetic dance and fanned herself with her hand.

"I know." Grant groaned and rubbed one of his knees. "And it's so ridiculous. I feel foolish out there, bouncing around like that. You're a bad influence on me...I'm getting too old to polka."

"Poor man." She flashed him a smile and patted his cheek...making Logan grit his teeth. Was it deliberate, knowing it would make him crazy? "You can't give up—we've been perfecting our style for twenty years."

"God save me." Steele brightened when he looked

past her to Logan, slouched against the wall. "Better yet, your husband-to-be will save me. The next one is all yours, Kincaid. I've done my time with the Red Bombshell."

"Thanks," Logan muttered.

Merrie laughed at her friend. Grant always complained, and she never paid any attention. "Not a chance, Grant. You'll never find such a proper stockbroker as Logan Kincaid doing the polka. You're stuck for the duration, buddy."

Logan caught her elbow and hauled her close. "You should try asking me to dance...I'd be delighted."

Surprise creased her forehead. "We've danced several times. What's wrong with you?"

"Nothing," he snapped.

Grant looked at them both, whistled beneath his breath and drawled something about rounding up his kids for the drive home.

"I'll see you next week," said Merrie.

"Actually I'll be over in the morning. I have some business with Paul."

She nodded, turned around to Logan, put her hands on her hips and scowled. "Now tell me, what's eating you? You've been acting funny all evening."

"Me?"

"Yes," Merrie said, exasperated. "You're all stiff and stuffy and won't talk to anyone. Not that it's unusual for you to act that way, but I thought you were changing...loosening up."

He snorted. "And I thought fiancée's normally spent more than five minutes at a time with the man they're engaged to marry. I must have been wrong about that."

"You...I..." Merrie gave a wordless shriek, turned on her heel and stalked from the barn.

How dare he?

A pretend engagement didn't give him exclusive rights. Even a *real* engagement wouldn't mean she had to ignore her responsibility as a hostess.

"Merrie, wait a minute."

She turned and glared. "What do you want?"

"I'm sorry. I shouldn't have said that part about our engagement."

"Darned right. I'm not your personal property. And in case you've forgotten, we *aren't* engaged. It's all a joke for your own private amusement. I knew I shouldn't have gone along with such a stupid idea."

"Okay." Logan made an obvious effort to calm down. "But I don't enjoy feeling jealous. I didn't expect you to play those kinds of games."

"Games?" Disbelief colored her voice.

"You were flirting with every man in the place. How did you expect me to feel?"

"I wasn't flirting, I was doing my job," she spat. "In case you hadn't noticed, I'm still an employee of the Bar Nothing. It's what I do—I make people feel at home. Help them relax. Sheesh! You're a real piece of work, Logan Kincaid."

"You and Grant—"

"Grant is like a big brother. We're friends, that's all. Besides, he's never gotten over losing his wife."

"Maybe I got carried away."

"No kidding?" Merrie crossed her arms over her stomach, blinking away angry tears. "You push and push, wanting to have your 'hot little affair.' But at the same time, you've made it crystal clear you have no intention of ever getting married, much less to someone like me."

"Try to understand," Logan said insistently. "Hell,

I'd never even seen a healthy marriage before I met your grandparents. I didn't think they existed.''

"I know. But under the circumstances, did you ever consider that you don't have any right feeling jealous? I've never made a secret of what I want—the ranch, a husband and a family. I was always honest about it. Why would I want to make you jealous?''

"Honey—''

"I'm not your honey, and leave me alone.'' She turned again, muttering beneath her breath.

Men. They were all alike. Rotten to the core. Lianne had been lucky, at least her fiancé was an obvious slime-ball, easy to identify and dump. Men like Logan could creep into your heart and tear it apart.

Still cursing to herself, Merrie walked up to the house and curled up on the porch swing. It was private there, hidden behind the morning glories twining their way to the roof.

Logan could go right back to Seattle for all she cared. She never wanted to see him again.

Logan clomped back to the barn dance. His ego had been wounded and he'd taken it out on Merrie. Again. But hell, she'd been so friendly with Grant. She must have known he was watching, and how it would make him feel.

"Logan?''

Great. It was Gloria Scott. He looked up, his patience at the breaking point.

"Yes?'' he barked.

"Where's Merrie? I need to talk to her.''

"Uh, I don't think she's feeling well. She went up to the house.''

"Oh." Gloria sidled around him. "That's too bad. I'll just check to see if she needs anything."

Terrific.

The last thing Merrie needed was a confrontation with Gloria Scott and her catty mouth. But he refused to feel responsible. The two women could duke it out, and he'd stay right down here, listening to the music and watching everyone dance.

His resolve lasted about sixty seconds. With a sigh of resignation, Logan turned and followed.

If nothing else, he could referee.

"Merrie?"

Merrie froze, unable to believe her rotten luck. She'd had all she could take—she was going to tell Gloria that her "engagement" with Logan was all a big fat lie, and wish her happy hunting. She might even help.

"Yes, Miss Scott?"

Gloria sniffed. "Logan said you weren't feeling well, only I really need someone to talk to, and I wondered if you didn't feel *too* bad..." Her voice trailed and she actually sounded miserable. *Really* miserable, not the hysteric sort of misery she'd been dishing out to everyone else.

Merrie looked at the other woman. Even in the darkness she could see the faint trace of tears. She groaned internally. "What's wrong?"

"I feel terrible coming up here like this. You've been so nice, and I've been so awful, but it's about Chip."

She blinked. "Chip?"

Gloria crumpled to the swing beside her. "I love him," she wailed. "And he won't marry me."

"Oh." Merrie shook her head, trying to clear it. She still hadn't been able to imagine Gloria and Chip having any kind of relationship, much less the kind that led to marriage. "Er, you've talked to him about it?"

"Over and over. I can't believe I fell in love with him. Daddy would never approve."

If it had been her, Merrie would have said "the heck with Daddy." But she wasn't Gloria. "Gosh, I'm afraid Chip isn't the marrying sort."

"Neither is Logan, and he proposed to you."

"Uh, yeah." Merrie closed her eyes in defeat. What was that old saying? About tangled webs and deception? "But that's different."

You'll never know how different.

"Actually, it was Daddy's idea about us getting married, because that way he'd never leave the company. Daddy was just so determined." Gloria sniffed again. "I know it wasn't nice of me, chasing Logan like that and upsetting his vacation. But it's okay now, because he's engaged to you and I don't have to worry about it anymore."

"Well, that's good," Merrie said, trying to sound sympathetic.

"To be honest," Gloria continued in a confidential tone. "Logan always scared me. He's so smart and intense about everything. He's much better off with you, because you're smart, too, and can talk to him about stuff."

Merrie bit the inside of her mouth to keep from asking what the society girl could possibly have in common with Chip, and what the two of *them* could ever talk about besides trading insults.

"I need someone more basic." Gloria's voice wobbled again. "Chip isn't complicated like Logan."

That was certainly true. Chip was *real* basic. Love was unpredictable. It was strange and stupid and made your heart do nutty things. Merrie should know, because she'd stupidly fallen in love with Logan, despite her best attempts to prevent it.

Tarnation.

She'd gone and admitted it to herself.

She was just as dumb as Gloria, falling for a man who didn't believe in marriage and lived in an entirely different world than herself.

Shaking her head wryly, Merrie patted the other woman's back as she wept. There wasn't much she could say. Chip wasn't about to give up his single life-style for anybody, much less a city woman with more money than sense. And even if her background wasn't a problem, most cowboys didn't make enough money to support a family.

"I don't know what to do," Gloria sobbed. "I'd even live in Montana, if that's what he wants."

Well, hell.

Merrie sighed. Gloria was still a twit. She lacked a backbone and couldn't tell one end of a horse from another. But she was kind of likable after all.

"Hi, Pidge."

Tucked into a narrow, hay filled space between the last horse stall and the barn wall, the gray cat hissed a warning.

"It's okay," Merrie soothed. "I'm not going to hurt them. I just want to look."

"So, you found where she's been hiding," commented Logan from behind her and she stiffened.

It had been easy to avoid Logan in the bustle of visitors saying goodbye and heading out in their respective vehicles. Gloria had gone, too, with many wistful backward looks at Chip. Merrie felt sorry for her, but she was certain the cowboy hadn't made any promises. He probably hadn't even been the aggressor. Chip had a laissez-faire attitude about women—he figured if he just waited around, they'd come to him.

"I've been wondering…how does a cat get a name like Pidge?" Warmth from Logan's body radiated through her as he crowded closer, ostensibly to look at the proud mama with her babies.

"Pidge has six toes on each foot," Merrie mumbled. "She looks pigeon-toed when she walks."

"Oh." Logan put his hand on Merrie's arm. He'd spent the entire night kicking himself for acting like an idiot.

Merrie was too compassionate and straightforward to ever do the hurtful things he'd seen happening between his parents. She had an essential sweetness…even Gloria had gone to her for comfort. He'd stood in the darkness beyond the porch, listening to the two women talk, and feeling ashamed. Merrie was a friendly, outgoing person who enjoyed people—that's what made her so successful as a wrangler.

"Honey, I was a big jerk," he said.

"Yes," she agreed baldly.

"I just keep feeling more and more…cornered."

Merrie sighed. "Cornered? This isn't a trap, Logan. You can leave anytime you want. Say the word and I'll fly you to the airport in Rapid City."

He stroked her arms with his hands, wanting to pull her against his chest and make everything all right. Except it wasn't all right, and he couldn't pretend otherwise. "You don't understand. The closer we get, the more I care about you. It scares the hell out of me, Merrie."

She was silent for so long, he didn't know if she was

angry or disgusted, or debating on ways to take his head off.

"How do you think I feel?" she said finally.

"At least you're more honest than I am."

Merrie laughed humorlessly. "Honest? I wasn't flirting with anyone last night. But deep down...I guess I was trying to make everything seem normal again. Treating all the guests the same, as though you weren't any more important than anyone else—pushing you away because it was safest."

"Why, Merrie?"

"Why?" She turned her head and looked at him incredulously. "You're a smart man, Logan. Figure it out. I don't want to choose between you and the ranch. And I don't want to spend the rest of my life loving someone who doesn't love me back."

"I'm sorry."

Getting to her feet, she edged past him to the center of the barn. "Keep your apologies. We let things get out of hand, and it's over. Go back to Seattle, and after a while I'll tell my grandparents that we broke things off."

"No."

Merrie looked at him warily.

"I may be slow and incredibly dense, but I'm not a coward. We've got to figure out what we feel for each other."

"I *know* how you feel, you already told me. Remember? I'm too...dramatic. Too emotional to be your kind of wife. Hell, I'm a *real* woman, that's your problem."

"For God's sake, Merrie. We were arguing. I said some irrational things."

"But deep down, that's how you think of me." She rubbed her temples, looking tired rather than angry. "Marriage is messy, Logan. It isn't a pristine house and quiet rooms. Do you think my grandparents never fight? They fight, and they make up, knowing eventually they're going to fight again.''

''But planning to—''

''No, *listen*. Unexpected things happen and you get into an argument. Not by plan. But you always plan to make up—because you know nothing in the world is more important than what you share together.''

A truck with a horse trailer pulled up outside the barn and a horn tooted. ''Merrie?'' called Grant Steele. ''I've got a surprise for you.''

''I'll be right there.'' Merrie looked at Logan for another long minute, pain etching her mouth.

''Honey…please.''

''No.'' She smiled sadly. ''Playtime is over—I have to get back to my life.''

Her quiet refusal shook Logan. He'd always gotten what he went after—from college, to a high-profile job, to the kind of financial security most people only dreamed about. But Merrie wasn't some kind of prize he could put on a shelf or count in a bank ledger. And she was determined to walk out of his world, as though she'd never touched it at all.

*His world…her world…*it was as though they lived on different planets.

Moodily he walked outside and watched Merrie. Was he the only one who noticed that her smile didn't reach her eyes, or that her natural sparkle was subdued?

''Your grandfather picked him out,'' Grant was saying as he opened the back of the horse trailer. ''As a birthday present. But we didn't want to bring him over while everyone was here…he's still rather excitable.''

He stepped inside, and emerged with a high-stepping stallion, gleaming a coppery red in the sunlight.

"Oh, Grant...he's beautiful."

"His name is Foxfire. He isn't fully broken, but I figured you could take things from here."

Merrie didn't say anything, but wonder and delight had softened the pain in her face. "Come here, beauty," she murmured in a low, firm tone, putting out a hand so the stallion could get her scent. The horse sniffed her fingers, then dipped his head for a rub on the face. Twelve hundred pounds of horseflesh, and he was putty in her hands.

"Morning, Kincaid," Grant said, leaning on a nearby fence. "Ever see anything like that? Merrie is a damned Pied Piper. If she wasn't so all-fired anxious to own the Bar Nothing, I'd hire her to break all my horses."

Logan spared him a deadly glance. "Don't even think about it."

Steele grinned. "She's a free agent. And I can't see Merrie promising to obey. Can you?"

"That's between Merrie and me."

Clucking softly to the horse, Merrie turned to lead him into the barn, when suddenly there was a frenzied commotion of a dog barking and feline hisses from within. A second later Bandit came streaking out in a flat run for the house.

The stallion reared, his nostrils flaring in alarm. He danced back on his hind legs, his forefeet pawing the air above Merrie's head.

God, no.

Logan dived forward, only to be sent rolling by a tackle from Grant Steele.

"Are you crazy?" Logan shouted. "He'll kill her!"

"Dammit, man, *look.*"

Merrie had let the long halter rope slide through her fingers, without releasing her grasp. And she'd already brought the stallion down again, though he continued to nervously step from side to side.

"Silly boy," she said, both soothing and gently scolding him at the same time. She went back to rubbing his face and neck as though nothing had happened. "That's just Bandit and Pidge. I'll bet Bandit wanted to say hi to her new babies, and Pidge didn't like it one single bit."

Foxfire cocked his head, listening as though he understood every word.

"You need to become friends with Bandit," Merrie continued, walking him toward the barn again. "We'll be working together out on the range, and he can teach you a lot."

The horse followed, as docile as a kitten.

"You're going to have heart failure if you keep overreacting," Grant said as he rose and dusted himself off. "There was nothing to worry about—Merrie's handled tougher situations with her eyes closed."

"She could have been hurt."

"This is a ranch, not a boutique. Get used to it."

"Get used to it?" Logan ground his teeth. "You're not in love with Merrie—you don't have anything to say about it. I'm not letting my wife get killed by some damned horse."

"What I'm saying," Steele said precisely, "is that Merrie won't ever *be* your wife if you can't live with the ranch. Now if you'll excuse me, I have work to do on my own spread." He called a goodbye to Merrie and climbed into his truck.

Dammit.

Logan slammed his fist into a fence post. The blow hurt, but not enough to absorb the adrenaline still racing through his veins. His heart had stopped when he'd seen that horse rearing over Merrie. She meant that much to him.

Everything.

She meant everything.

And he was a blasted fool for not seeing it before. If anything happened to Merrie he might as well crawl into a hole and die, too, because he surely wouldn't want to keep breathing. He didn't want her in danger, not ever again.

Logan went to the barn and looked inside—Merrie had put Foxfire into a stall and she was wiping a soft cloth over his body. The entire time she kept talking, in a voice as smooth and warm as mulled wine. The incident in the yard had been nothing out of the ordinary…just another day's work.

His jaw tightened.

I don't want to choose between you and the ranch.

Lord, when it came right down to it, he didn't want her to choose, either. The Bar Nothing was part of Merrie—as much a part of her identity as her name or smile. Take away that dream…and she wouldn't be the woman he loved.

But how could he live each day, knowing the dangers she would face? And what about his plans…his goal to live in New York? It didn't seem very appealing anymore, yet he wasn't certain that moving to Montana was the answer.

After long minutes of wanting her to say something…*anything,* Merrie finally looked up and smiled faintly. "Were you and Grant playing football? Or just being clumsy?"

He should have realized she'd seen Steele's tackle. Not too much got past her. "He was running interference. Seems I thought you needed help, and he disagreed."

"He was right."

"Yeah. I kind of figured that out."

Merrie rubbed Foxfire's nose. "You're just like Grand-dad. You think a woman can't handle ranch work."

"That's not what I think, and I'm not sure your grand-father does, either. Honey, did you ever imagine that he was just protecting you? Or maybe he was just protecting himself, because he didn't want to see you get hurt?"

"I don't need protecting."

Logan clenched his fists. She was a damned stubborn woman. "Maybe you don't, but a decent man protects his family. What if you were pregnant? Do you think your husband should let you dive into a stampede or rush out in a blizzard to feed the cattle?"

She glared at him. "*Let* me?"

"You know what I meant."

"Huh. I want a partnership, not a castle to live in."

Merrie lifted Foxfire's legs one by one to clean his hooves. Logan knew it was to get him accustomed to her touch and scent. His mouth twisted ironically. He'd been captured the same way...by touch and scent, by laughter and warmth and a need so strong it tore him apart.

Pain lanced through Logan's head and he sighed. When everything was said and done, he wanted Merrie to have her dream, even if he couldn't share it with her.

"Honey, where's your grandfather?"

She looked at him warily. "He went for a ride out toward the airstrip. Why?"

What was that old gag—*I need to see a man about a horse?* Or in this case, he needed to see Paul Harding about a ranch. "Just some business. I want to discuss...cattle futures with him."

"Futures? Is that some kind of stockbroker term?"

"Yeah," Logan muttered. "Exactly." He led Dust Devil from his stall and quickly saddled him.

He and Dust Devil had become good friends, and the horse gently snorted and nudged his chest, hoping for a carrot.

"Just a minute, boy." Logan went to the half-whiskey barrel where apples and carrots were kept as equine treats…the Bar Nothing didn't overlook the smallest detail. Or rather, Merrie didn't. The wranglers had told him she returned to the ranch every year, bubbling with ideas for improvements. Paul Harding apparently hadn't figured out that his granddaughter was the reason the dude ranch had become so wildly successful…and Logan planned to tell him.

"My offer is still open," Merrie said after he'd fed the carrot to Dust Devil, then mounted up.

"What offer?"

"To fly you out."

Logan smiled grimly. There was some comfort in knowing he wasn't the only one confused and worried about the future. "No, thanks. I still have two weeks left of my vacation…and I plan to spend every minute of them here in Montana."

"It would be smarter to leave."

"Not a chance, honey. Not one damn chance."

"Merrie says I'm old-fashioned and hardheaded, and that's why I won't sell her the ranch," commented Paul Harding as he rode his horse alongside Logan.

"Is that why, sir?"

"Nope." The older man fingered the reins for a long minute. "I love all my grandchildren," he said finally. "But Merrie…she's different. She has a feel for the land."

"So why haven't you been willing to sell her the Bar Nothing?" Logan asked grimly. "Of anyone, *you* should understand how important it is to her. You should have agreed to the sale a long time ago."

Paul smiled faintly. "Son, I love this ranch, but it won't hold you when you're grieving, or rejoice with your blessings. It's hard enough for a man to find someone who'll pull up roots to share his life…and damned near impossible for a woman—the world may be changing, but it hasn't changed that much. Things might have been different if she'd married Grant Steele. But they never felt that way about each other."

"Oh."

Suddenly everything became a lot clearer to Logan. Paul Harding didn't distrust Merrie's ability to run the ranch, he just didn't want her to be alone. "Well, that's not so much of a worry now, is it?" he said, somewhat uncomfortably.

Harding regarded him shrewdly. "I'm not a dang fool, son. You talked her into that story about gettin' married, didn't you? Got her to go along somehow."

Logan sighed. This conversation wasn't going the way he'd planned. He just wanted to give Merrie the collateral she needed for the ranch. No strings attached. No balloon payments or foreclosure hanging over her head.

Hell, Logan would never let anything happen to Merrie *or* the Bar Nothing. If push came to shove, he could find a hundred investors willing to back them up. Not all of his clients were obnoxious. When he thought about it, a lot of them were pretty darned nice. And they enjoyed new and different kinds of investment opportunities.

"What do you have to say for yourself?" Harding prompted.

"You're right, the engagement wasn't real," Logan

said quietly. "It started off as a joke, and got out of control. But I'm in love with your granddaughter, and I think she's in love with me. Except we don't have a prayer of sorting things out while she's worried about the Bar Nothing's future."

Logan stared into the distance, seeing more than just the horizon. "You've said you wanted to retire, and I have enough collateral to cover the purchase price. I'd like you to agree to let Merrie take over management at the end of the summer."

"And if you don't 'sort' things out?"

A sick sensation twisted in Logan's gut. *No.* He couldn't lose Merrie. "Well, I guess you'll have to trust me on that one. And you'll have to trust Merrie. She deserves a shot at the Bar Nothing, whether we end up together or not."

Chapter Ten

"Logan Kincaid! What did you think you were doing?"

The question woke Logan from a much-needed nap, and he yawned. Merrie could sure pack a lot of volume for such a little thing. "Something wrong, honey?"

"Yeah...you made a deal with Granddad."

Logan lifted himself on his elbows. He'd gone up to the slope behind the ranch house, trying to sort things out in his head.

It hadn't taken long.

If it came to a choice between Merrie and anything else, he'd choose Merrie. In a way, the choice had already been made days ago. He could play the stock market on a computer when they weren't busy with the ranch. With so much modern technology available, you didn't have to live in New York to deal on Wall Street.

Then he'd fallen asleep, more content than he ever remembered feeling. He should have known it wouldn't be that easy.

"What about it? That's what you wanted, to buy the Bar Nothing. I just nudged things along a little."

"You have no right interfering. This is my life. Jeez, I can't believe you'd go behind my back like that!"

The muscles in Logan's body tightened and he climbed to his feet. "I didn't go behind your back—at least not the way you seem to think. I wanted you to have your dream. Why are you so upset?"

"Why?" Merrie threw out her hands, her face white and strained. "You don't get it, do you? I've been working my entire life for this, and now, because a *man* walks in with a ton of money and the right set of chromosomes, Granddad decides he can trust 'us' with the ranch."

"I do 'get' it." Logan reminded himself not to get angry. "Honey, it wasn't because he didn't trust you."

"Sure. That's why he decided he could sell me the ranch after he thought we were engaged. A big strong man to take care of things."

"No. A *partner.* That's all he wanted...for you to have someone of your own. Not because he didn't trust you, but because he didn't want you to spend your life alone here."

"It wouldn't have happened that way."

"No?" Logan caught Merrie's shoulders and shook her gently. "You're so single-minded and stubborn you can't see anything but the Bar Nothing."

"What am I supposed to see?" she asked sarcastically.

"Me, honey. *Me.*"

"Oh, right." Her chest rose and fell with ragged breaths of air. "The stockbroker. The man who doesn't believe in marriage. The man who wants to live in New York."

"And the man who's so crazy about you he's willing to argue this stupid argument. Don't forget that one."

"Terrific. I'm stupid."

Damnation. It was hard not to get angry. Merrie was so blasted stubborn she wasn't hearing anything he was saying. "Sweetheart, you're a beautiful, intelligent woman, but you don't *listen.*"

"What am I supposed to hear? All the logical reasons I can't manage the ranch by myself?"

"Hell," Logan cursed, losing his tenuous hold on his temper. "You talk about wanting a partner in your marriage, but you're not interested in a partnership. You want to get the ranch by yourself, then drop some poor sap into it like the cherry on top of an ice-cream sundae."

"That's insulting," Merrie snapped.

"For the man it certainly is. Well, honey, I'm not playing it your way. What if I want it all?"

She looked at him uncertainly. "All what?"

"Both. A partnership and a marriage. With you. On the Bar Nothing. And you're going to have to make up that pigheaded mind of yours, because I'm not going to take anything less."

Merrie shook her head, so confused she could hardly think. "I don't believe that."

"Well, believe this."

Logan caught her tight and hard against him, kissing her mouth like a hawk falling on prey. He wasn't wooing, he was demanding...with all the pent-up fury of denied passion and anger, and the pain of thoughtless words both spoken and received.

A moan welled from Merrie's chest and was lost in the assault upon her senses. How could you think clearly in the middle of so much heat?

As though remembering his greater strength, Logan's hold lightened, his hands stroking up and down her back, urging her closer of her own accord.

"Logan, no," she sighed, her words lost in the sultry warmth of his kiss, and the satin glide of his tongue, thrusting deeper and deeper between her lips.

Somehow, she had to make sense of the confusion raging inside her head, and she broke away. Shivering, despite the heat of the day and aching with so much emotion she hardly knew herself.

"Merrie...come back," Logan said hoarsely, his eyes so dark with emotion they looked black, even in the sunlight.

She put her fingers to her mouth. "I can't...I have to think."

Merrie stumbled away, and by the time she reached the barn she was running. Sun Spot was tied to the corral, waiting patiently for the ride that had been postponed by her grandfather's news. She untied him and fitted her foot into the stirrup.

Sun Spot loved to gallop and she gave him his head. Her hair came free from its loose confinement, and she bent over the palomino's neck, letting her body move with the powerful animal.

You can't see anything but the Bar Nothing.

The accusation had angered her, but mostly because it was true. She'd *had* to focus all her attention, all her energy on getting the ranch. It was the only way to earn the down payment, of proving her determination to her grandfather. And all through those years, what had frightened her about falling in love was the possibility of losing the ranch. Yet love was part of her dream...children and a husband who loved her dearly.

Logan had said he was crazy about her, but he hadn't said he loved her. "Crazy" might translate to sex, more than love. There was no doubt he wanted her with a volcanic intensity—she wanted him the same way.

"Tarnation," Merrie groaned, finally pulling Sun Spot to a halt. She'd instinctively headed for her favorite place on the ranch...the hill where she'd taken Logan that first day.

She sat, breathing hard with Sun Spot, and staring up at the rocky outcropping. Memories of Logan's caresses and urgent words echoed in her ears.

You want to get the ranch by yourself, then drop some poor sap into it like the cherry on top of an ice-cream sundae.

"*No.*"

Merrie didn't even realize she'd spoken the word aloud until Sun Spot moved restlessly, and she patted his neck, soothing him. She'd always known she would have to marry a man who was interested in the ranch...someone who wanted to make it his home. But not the way Logan had made it sound. Right? Not calculated and cold-blooded. Not possessively.

Yet when she remembered the accusations she'd thrown at him, Merrie muttered another curse. Logan had every right to be angry and disgusted.

"What am I going to do?" she whispered.

If Logan loved her...then he had to be hurt, wondering if the ranch was more important than him.

What if I want it all? A partnership and a marriage?

Not exactly a proposal, but clear enough to know what he wanted...what he intended.

Merrie wrapped her arms around her stomach and moaned. Despite all her attempts to protect herself, she was going to have to choose between Logan and the ranch. He had too much pride to stay for long in Montana, always questioning how much she cared for him. She couldn't even blame him...the same question would torment her if the situation was reversed.

They couldn't live on her dreams alone. Marriage meant compromise. It wasn't one person getting everything, and the other going along.

What should she do?

Merrie lifted her head and looked around at the surrounding countryside. If she chose Logan, it wouldn't belong to her anymore. This land had sheltered her family for more than a century. Their homestead had been the first permanent structure. Generations of Hardings rested in a small cemetery west of the house. What would those Hardings decide if they had to choose?

Then...without any more thought, Merrie knew.

Logan.

Despite the sweat and toil, the history of their blood written upon the land...they'd choose love.

Because without love, the land meant nothing.

"Tell me something," Merrie said as she slowly walked up to the ranch house. Logan was sitting on the porch steps and her feet faltered. He was solid and real, and his face was grim as he looked at her, waiting for a response.

"What?"

"Would you have come to Montana, if you'd known how things were going to turn out?" she asked.

A wry smile curved his mouth. "I think that depends on the next few minutes...and what you're going to tell me. Not that I intend to give up, you understand."

"Of course not."

"I'm just as stubborn as you are, and don't forget it."

"I know." Merrie put her hands into her pockets and shrugged. She was good at breaking horses and running a dude ranch, not at romance. Until she'd met Logan it had been easy to avoid entanglement. None of the men she'd met had ever tempted her. But Logan…he was electric. *No*body could ignore Logan Kincaid, at least not a woman under ninety.

The ranch had isolated her from the turmoil and dangers of falling in love. And the joy. She couldn't forget that part, though up till now, falling in love had been pretty traumatic. It certainly wasn't all roses and romantic candlelight.

"Well, honey?" he prompted gently. "I may not be the best husband prospect, but I'm willing to let go of my past…all those fears about getting married. What about you? Can you share that dream you've wanted for so long?"

"I…" The words stuck in her throat. He still hadn't said he loved her. But she loved him. *Terribly.* So much it scared the living daylights out of her. "What about me being the wrong kind of woman? I'm not sophisticated or blond, or any of that stuff."

He reached out a long arm and took her hand in his. By comparison, her fingers were small and delicate…but a long way from manicured perfection. You couldn't be manicured on a ranch. Merrie wasn't even sure she could manage it in New York, no matter how hard she tried. She wasn't made for cocktail parties and designer clothing.

Logan laced their fingers together and tugged until she stood between his outstretched legs. He was so tall their eyes were almost at the same level, though he remained seated on the step.

"Honey, I would have hated a woman from Sully's wife list. Tall and blond?" He shrugged and touched a lock of her windblown auburn hair. "That was immature—a holdover from leering at the high school cheerleader in her miniskirts. I much prefer hair the color of cinnamon, and someone who fits against my heart as though we'd been made for each other.''

''But—''

''As for reserved, composed and elegant?'' he continued as though she hadn't said anything. ''That was because I thought of Grace Kelly. She always looked distant and unattainable, and since I didn't want a wife anyway, unattainable seemed like a good idea.''

''You could have anyone you want,'' Merrie muttered.

''Flattering, but not true.'' His thumb traced circles over her palm and she trembled. ''Now let's see… sophisticated. There are all kinds of sophistication…like a woman who appreciates people just the way they are. A woman who can be compassionate to someone like Gloria Scott, even when she's hurting inside herself.''

''Oh.'' Warmth burned in Merrie's face. Yet a secret pleasure was growing inside her. ''You heard us talking.''

''Yeah, I heard. You were sweet and kind, even though Gloria doesn't deserve anything from you.''

''She was upset. I think she really loves Chip.''

''That would be a miracle.'' But his voice wasn't caustic, just amused. ''Honey…don't you see? That list was about *not* getting married. It wasn't about us.''

''What about me being too emotional?''

He urged her closer, pulling till she was sitting on his hard thigh. She squirmed a little, because the pressure on her fanny made sultry sensations dart through her veins and settle deep in her tummy. And from his smile, she knew Logan understood exactly what it did to her. His large hand settled over her abdomen, massaging the affected area and making it worse.

"Logan," she said desperately. "I don't think you should do that."

"Oh…" He smiled wickedly. "I definitely think I should. You see, that's part of you being emotional…knowing you want me, and being unable to hide what you feel. You're so incredibly honest, Merrie. Especially the way you respond to me." His expression sobered and he kissed her throat. "That was the problem between my parents—they were so busy playing games and hurting each other, they never took the time to be honest."

"I'm not sure how honest I am," she muttered. "It seems I keep doing things for certain reasons, and realizing later that the reasons were completely different."

"That's okay. We all do it—that's human nature."

Merrie relaxed into Logan's chest. As a junior high school science teacher, she knew a lot about biology. She saw budding biology at work in her students, and she knew about the scientific processes. But none of that could explain why the feel of his heat-dampened body could make her breath short and nerves jumpy with sensual awareness.

"I love you," she whispered.

Logan jerked. "What did you say?"

"I love you," she said quickly, sitting up straight again. "And I'll live in Seattle or New York, if that's what you want. I can't promise to really fit into that big city life-style, but I'll try. So…are you going to marry me or what?"

Logan looked at Merrie, her chin raised stubbornly in the air, ready for his rejection if that's what was coming. He didn't know if he should laugh or shake her.

"Of course we're going to get married. I happen to love you, too," he drawled.

"You do?" The shattering joy and delight in her green eyes humbled him. Never in his life had he imagined such a woman, so full of life and courage. And she belonged to him, the way he belonged to her.

"I absolutely adore you," Logan vowed. "I've just been too stubborn to admit it. If I hadn't found you on that tree house, I would have spent the rest of my life being miserable. I've already made a bundle of money, but it would never have been enough."

"Your scorecard," Merrie said quietly.

"Yes. A scorecard...get so many points, and then I'd be happy. Only by the time I'd made those points, the rules would have changed, and I'd need to make more. You understood what I was trying to do, even when I didn't."

She winced and bit her lip. "Yeah, but haven't I been doing the same thing with the ranch?"

He stroked his thumb across her mouth, his eyes tender. "There are some dreams worth fighting for...and the Bar Nothing is one of them. I want to raise our kids here. It's a wonderful heritage, Merrie. You were right about that."

"Children?" she breathed.

"Yeah...a bunch. Any objections?"

She shook her head vigorously. "No."

"Good. But you'll have to be careful when you're pregnant, and not overdo," he warned. "I'm going to be very old-fashioned about that. Actually I want you to be careful all the time, but especially when you're having a baby."

"I can already tell, you're going to be a worrywart. Pregnancy doesn't incapacitate a woman," Merrie argued. But she didn't look *too* upset, more amused.

"Honey! I'm not joking."

"Okay, I'll be careful." Even though she'd agreed, Logan knew he'd have to watch her. She was too blasted independent.

"Good. And we're not living in the city," he ordered. "I *hate* the city. It's a terrible place to raise kids."

Merrie squirmed some more on his lap and he groaned. He finally caught her hips to hold her still.

"You don't hate the city," she insisted. "I remember perfectly. You said you hated small towns."

"The Bar Nothing isn't a small town."

"It isn't the city, either."

"That's right."

She drew back, puzzled. "I don't understand."

"The truth is I never really liked big cities. They just seemed better than a small community where people gossip and know everything about you. And cities are easier places to make a name for yourself...easier to prove I wasn't just some second-rate kid from the wrong side of town."

Merrie framed his face in her hands and kissed him lightly, *lovingly,* on the lips. "You don't have to prove anything. Not to me. Not ever. And you were *never* second-rate. Do you hear me, Logan Kincaid?"

A wild freedom expanded in Logan's chest. He'd never have to prove himself to Merrie. She loved and believed in him, and that was all he'd ever need.

"I hear you. And we *are* living in Montana," he said for good measure. "I don't want any argument about it."

"Me? Argue?"

"Yeah, you. The Red Bombshell."

"Not a chance."

"Hmm." Logan lifted Merrie and carried her to the porch swing. Several cowboys were working around the corrals and he wanted some privacy to kiss her properly.

"I suppose we're going to have some terrific arguments," he murmured, cuddling her close.

Her smile was slow and slumberous with desire, and it made him ache with need and tenderness, all at the same time. "Is that so?"

"Yup. You're not a redhead for nothing."

"My hair isn't red."

"See what I mean?"

She laughed, though her eyes were questioning. "Aren't you worried about that? About the fighting?"

"Nope." Logan tugged a strand of her bright hair. "Not anymore. Because someone told me the trick is planning to make up. And I have this idea...about the best way to make up." He nudged her collar to one side and kissed her shoulder.

"I think I'm going to like this idea," she said thickly.

"Of course we'll have to experiment." Logan kissed her again, moving downward, dispensing with the buttons with his usual efficiency. "Test the best ways to resolve our disagreements. Practice, practice...practice. But I'm willing to work at it."

There was a loud "harrumph" from behind them, and Merrie wiggled upward to look over his shoulder, one hand gathering her shirt together. "Hi, Granddad... Grandma. Logan and I were just...talking."

Logan stifled a laugh and she poked him.

"I suppose you'll be wanting another engagement party," her grandmother said, her hands on her hips.

"Uh, why should I want that?" she asked, feeling guilty. "We already had an engagement party."

"This one will be different." Eva Harding tried to look stern. "A real party for a real engagement. I presume you're actually engaged this time. Aren't you? Or does your grandfather have to pull out the shotgun?"

"I thought they didn't 'do' shotgun weddings anymore," Logan whispered, brushing her hands to one side while he helped fasten her buttons. He lifted her jaw, which had dropped at her grandmother's cool announcement.

"You knew?" Merrie gasped.

"Of course they knew, honey," said Logan. "These are intelligent people we're dealing with."

"But you never said anything, Granddad. You agreed to sell us the ranch."

Paul Harding shrugged apologetically. "Your young man is right, Merrie-girl. I should have agreed to sell you the Bar Nothing a long time ago."

"Then you knew we weren't really engaged," she said faintly. "This afternoon...when you told me about your agreement."

"I knew. Logan and I had already discussed the matter."

Merrie's gaze locked with Logan's. "Why didn't you tell me?"

"I tried, honey. *Believe me.* But you weren't in a listening mood."

Merrie thought back, realizing she hadn't given him a chance to explain anything. She'd been furious and unreasonable. It was a wonder he hadn't gotten scared off completely. "Sorry."

"That's okay." He grinned his heart-stopping grin. "Everything turned out all right."

"Then you *are* engaged?" Eva Harding prodded. "For real this time?"

Merrie kissed her fiancé. "Yes, Grandma. We're engaged."

"And it took *twelve whole days* to make up your mind," Logan teased. "Seven days longer than your grandparents. I'll have fun telling the children about that.''

They shared a secret loving look.

''Amongst other things,'' she whispered.

Epilogue

"Is this everything, honey?"

Merrie smiled at her husband as he worked setting up the tent. It was their fifth anniversary, and they were spending it camping on her special hill. He pounded the last stake into the ground and flipped both ends open to catch the evening breeze.

"We don't need a lot of supplies. We're only going to be here overnight," she reminded him.

Logan snapped a blanket out on the ground. "I know. Get over here, woman," he ordered in a mock parody of masculine dominance...followed by an endearing grin. "I don't want to waste any of our valuable time."

Smiling, she sat snugly cradled in his arms and watched as the sun set behind the Western horizon. It was July 1, and they wouldn't have a lot of time for private celebrating before their next group of guests arrived. The Fourth of July was a big holiday at the Bar Nothing.

Five years.

She could hardly believe so much time had gone by. Yet they'd been happy years. Logan loved working the ranch with her, and if he was a little overprotective, it wasn't unmanageable. There were worse things than having your husband want to protect his family.

"It's so warm out," she murmured. "I don't know why you insisted on bringing one of the tents."

Logan smiled into Merrie's hair. She rested against his chest, her head tucked under his chin. "Just fulfilling a fantasy."

She turned her head to look at him. "With a tent?"

"Mmm. Remember that first day we got to Montana?"

"Vividly."

He chuckled. "I thought *tents?* How could you have a romantic rendezvous in a tent, surrounded by other tents? I was very frustrated."

"So you want to make love in a tent."

"Yup. You *are* planning to be warm and willing in my sleeping bag tonight, aren't you?"

"Aren't I warm and willing all the time?"

"Mmm…yes." There was a wealth of sensual satisfaction in his voice. "You raise warm and willing to an art form."

Logan snuggled his wife closer and smiled again. Who would have thought that two little words like "I do" could make him so happy? Merrie had entered his life with the force of a tidal wave, and nothing had changed. She still swept everyone along with her enthusiasm, at the same time managing to be a wonderful wife and mother. As for himself…he'd discovered a life more rewarding than he could possibly have imagined.

Merrie and the children made all the difference in the world. Four-year-old Jennie was a miniature version of her mother—energy and all. And they could hardly keep

Kent in the house. Though only eighteen months old, he was fascinated with horses, and not the least bit intimidated by creatures so much larger than himself. He got that from his mother, too.

"Mmm…I forgot to tell you we got another reservation for the Fourth," Merrie said. "It came in on the fax machine this afternoon. Guess who's coming?"

At her droll tone, Logan groaned. "Not Gloria."

"Yup. I think she may be wearing Chip down…he actually looked glad when I told him."

"Cowed is more like it, poor guy."

"Stop that. Gloria really loves Chip."

"Yeah, she loves him the way a wolf loves lamb chops. I can't imagine those two married."

"You couldn't imagine yourself married, either," his wife said tartly, nudging him with her elbow.

It was undeniably true. "Okay," he conceded. "But Chip doesn't have my advantage."

"And what advantage would that be?"

"He doesn't have you."

"Huh," Merrie mumbled, her face stained pink by more than the sunset.

Logan chuckled. He loved her ability to still blush after five years of passionate marriage, but mostly he loved her. Completely and utterly. Not that they didn't fight. Hell, they had some terrific battles—sometimes over silly things, and sometimes for important reasons. But marrying her had been the best move of his life.

"By the way, your grandmother sent something along to help us celebrate." Logan reached inside the tent and pulled out a bottle of champagne. "It was nice of them to watch the kids for us," he added.

"Nice nothing. They love taking care of Jennie and Kent, and they spoil them shamefully." Merrie held the glasses while he popped the cork. "I'm surprised they haven't moved back to Montana, just to play with their great-grandchildren."

"Eva was hinting about us having another baby," Logan said, grinning. He glanced significantly at her flat tummy. "And I couldn't help remembering this was a fertile time of the month for you."

Merrie dipped her finger in her champagne and flicked it at him. "You've gotten awfully knowledgeable about fertility and such...for a slicker."

Logan chuckled. "It comes in handy. So what do you say about starting number three?"

"Well..." She arched her neck and licked drops of splattered wine from his chin. "I'd hate to put your expertise to waste, so I guess the answer is yes."

"A woman after my heart," he drawled, giving her a long, heated kiss, his hands roaming over her breasts and stomach with growing urgency.

Merrie popped the snap on Logan's jeans and played with the zipper, smiling at his sudden intake of breath. "That's not all I'm after."

"Honey, whatever you want, as long as you want it," he promised.

"Wonderful," she purred. "I've got a lot of energy to work off."

With Logan's eager cooperation, they shimmied backward into the tent, spilling champagne on the sleeping bag, and laughing because it didn't matter. Then Merrie wasn't laughing, because Logan's heart was in his eyes, looking at her with the kind of sizzling intensity most women only dreamed about.

"Happy fifth anniversary," she whispered. "I love you."

"That's good because you're not getting rid of me. I'll

be around for another fifty years or so...chasing cattle and children around the place. And of course *you*."

"Of course," she agreed.

"It won't be nearly long enough," Logan said softly. "So you'd better get used to it."

And as he bent to kiss her, Merrie knew this was one cowboy she was keeping.

* * * * *

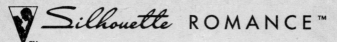

Silhouette ROMANCE™

SOMETIMES THE SMALLEST PACKAGES CAN LEAD TO THE BIGGEST SURPRISES!

Join *Silhouette Romance*
as more couples experience
the joy only babies
can bring!

Bundles of Joy

July 1999
BABIES, RATTLES AND CRIBS... OH MY!
by Leanna Wilson (SR #1378)

His baby girl had suddenly appeared on his doorstep, and Luke Crandall needed daddy lessons—fast! So lovely Sydney Reede agreed to help the befuddled bachelor. But when baby cuddles turned into grown-up kisses, Sydney wondered if what Luke really wanted was *her!*

August 1999
THE BILLIONAIRE AND THE BASSINET
by Suzanne McMinn (SR #1384)

When billionaire Garrett Blakemore set out to find the truth about a possible heir to his family's fortune, he didn't expect to meet a pretty single mom and her adorable baby! But the more time he spent with Lanie Blakemore and her bundle of joy, the more he found himself wanting the role of dad....

And look for more **Bundles of Joy** titles in late 1999:

THE BABY BOND by Lilian Darcy (SR #1390)
in September 1999

BABY, YOU'RE MINE by Lindsay Longford (SR #1396)
in October 1999

Available at your favorite retail outlet.

Silhouette®

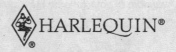

Coming in June 1999 from
Silhouette® Books...

Those matchmaking folks at Gulliver's Travels are at
it again—and look who they're working their magic
on this time, in

HOLIDAY
Honeymoons

Two Tickets to Paradise

For the first time anywhere, enjoy these two new
complete stories in one sizzling volume!

HIS FIRST FATHER'S DAY   **Merline Lovelace**
A little girl's search for her father leads her to
Tony Peretti's front door...and leads *Tony* into the
arms of his long-lost love—the child's mother!

MARRIED ON THE FOURTH   **Carole Buck**
Can summer love turn into the real thing? When
it comes to Maddy Malone and Evan Blake's
Independence Day romance, the answer is a
definite "yes!"

Don't miss this brand-new release—
HOLIDAY HONEYMOONS: Two Tickets to Paradise—
coming June 1999, only from Silhouette Books.

Available at your favorite retail outlet.

*This June 1999, the legend
continues in Jacobsville*

Diana Palmer

LONG, TALL TEXANS
EMMETT, REGAN & BURKE

This June 1999, Silhouette brings readers
an extra-special trade-size collection
for Diana Palmer's legion of fans.
These three favorite Long, Tall Texans
stories have been brought back in
one collectible trade-size edition.

*Emmett, Regan & Burke are about to be led
down the bridal path by three irresistible women.
Get ready for the fireworks!*

**Don't miss this collection of favorite
Long, Tall Texans stories…
available in June 1999
at your favorite retail outlet.**

**Then in August 1999 watch for
LOVE WITH A LONG, TALL TEXAN
a trio of brand-new short stories featuring
three irresistible Long, Tall Texans.**

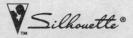